Tardy Pass, No Questions Asked

One guidance counselor. One science teacher. Zero chance it stays professional.

A Prequel to the Marchfield Middle Series

M. Jayne LaDow

To Megan and Miles—
Because of you, I listen better, love deeper, and see more clearly. Thank you for leading the way.

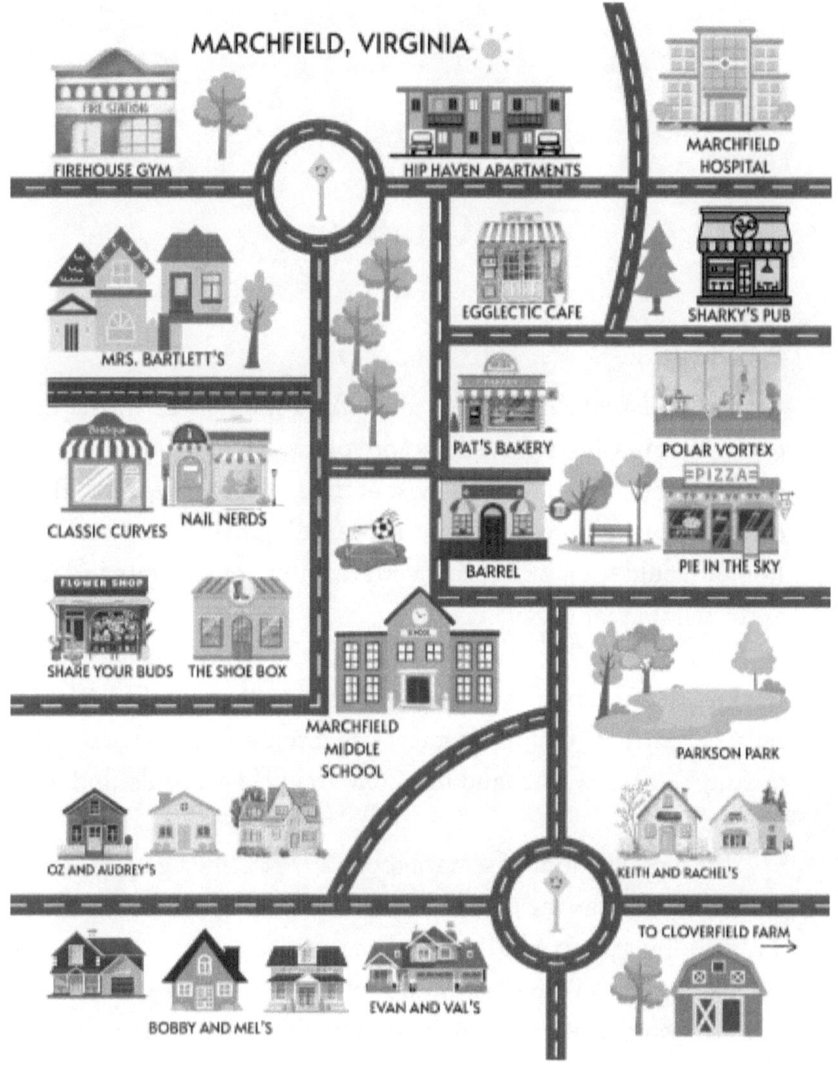

MARCHFIELD, VIRGINIA
FIREHOUSE GYM
HIP HAVEN APARTMENTS
MARCHFIELD HOSPITAL
MRS. BARTLETT'S
EGGLECTIC CAFE
SHARKY'S PUB
CLASSIC CURVES
NAIL NERDS
PAT'S BAKERY
POLAR VORTEX
BARREL
PIE IN THE SKY
SHARE YOUR BUDS
THE SHOE BOX
MARCHFIELD MIDDLE SCHOOL
PARKSON PARK
OZ AND AUDREY'S
KEITH AND RACHEL'S
TO CLOVERFIELD FARM
BOBBY AND MEL'S
EVAN AND VAL'S

Chapter 1

Bobby

Marchfield Middle stood like a monument in the heart of town, its imposing red brick façade softened by the ivy that had crept along the mortar longer than most of the staff had been alive. The wide, empty hallways were quiet, and the building held a sense of anticipation. It would soon be buzzing with the noise of students and teachers as the school year began.

Maybe it was because of my time in the Army, but I couldn't help but love the structure and rhythm of public education. This place had a pulse, a heartbeat that made it feel safe. Even if I was the new kid—just starting out as a teacher and new to Marchfield—I could find my footing here

The wooden door of science room 207 felt like a gateway to my future. I would cross the threshold and begin the next chapter mentoring and molding young minds in my first real classroom.

I stopped to take it in, trying to calm my jittery excitement. The numbers on the plaque were worn, like they'd been there forever, just like this school. The thrill of it was almost overwhelming.

I pulled out my phone and started a video for my friend, Oz. He'd begun his first day in New York yesterday.

"Hey, man. This is it. Room 207. Let's see what's inside." I grabbed the doorknob with shaky fingers, then twisted.

Nothing.

"Are you kidding me?" I muttered, stopping the video. The humidity from the summer had probably swollen the wood.

Leaning into the door, I pressed my shoulder against it for leverage. The door wouldn't open. Either it was stuck or staging a quiet protest.

Scanning for witnesses to my increasingly pathetic struggle, I glanced up and down the hallway. A few teachers strolled by, lost in their own worlds, probably not even noticing the new kid flailing at the door like an overenthusiastic puppy.

I sighed, then tried once more, twisting the knob and pushing with everything I had, but it wouldn't budge.

No one told me I'd need a key, but since beating on the door wasn't working, I'd head to the office to ask.

A moment later, I walked into Marchfield Middle's administration area, a maze of narrow hallways, small conference rooms, and postage stamp sized offices. I'd been escorted into the principal's office when I'd interviewed, and at the time, the administrative assistants had been seated in the middle at two desks. Unfortunately, they were empty now.

Taking the corridor to the right, I turned a corner and spotted a door slightly ajar, I hesitated for a moment, listening. Quiet, humming drifted through the stillness of the space around me. I followed it.

The door to the records room was open, the small space filled with filing cabinets, their metal surfaces gleaming in the low light. A woman pulled files from a drawer, adding them to a tall teetering stack on a chair beside her. With her back to me, she flipped through some documents, still humming, completely unaware of my presence.

I froze. It was like a punch to my gut. Her hair, the color of cinnamon, fell just past her shoulders in waves. Her trim body and rounded butt hinted at the softness beneath her simple fitted shirt and black pants.

Were her lips painted dark red to match the highlights in her hair? A strong urge to spin her around and see gripped me, along with the sharp desire to pressed my lips to hers. My pulse quickened, and I couldn't help but wonder if the pressure of her kiss would be gentle or hungry—if she would take control or if I would.

What the hell? I shook myself out of the daydream. I needed to get a grip. I didn't even know this woman, and I was melting like a tween at a boy band concert.

Stick to the mission, Bobby. Get your key. Then ask for the woman's number.

Clearing my throat, I stepped forward, and she jumped and spun towards me. I flinched instinctively, hands half-raised like I might catch her.

Or apologize with jazz hands.

"Sorry, didn't mean to—"

She flung her hands out, her right hand jostling the chair with the towering stack of files. As the papers began to sway, she took a quick step back—just as the strap of her sandal gave a dramatic crack. Her ankle twisted, balance vanished, and she tumbled with a yelp, sending files flying like startled pigeons.

I leaped forward, trying to stop the avalanche of paper before it could slide off the chair, but the woman staggered forward.

"Those are confidential files!"

My momentum propelled me forward, crashing into her as the pile of folders wobbled and fell. We staggered together in a tangled flail of limbs, bumping into the chair as papers fluttered around our feet like confetti at the world's least coordinated parade.

The files sliced through the air, the sound of their sharp edges hissing as they landed with a resigned thud. Test scores, report cards, and school photos scattered across the tile floor.

"Oof!" I grunted, grasping her shoulders to steady her. "Guess I'm not making a smooth first impression."

She blinked, wide-eyed, before her gaze flickered over me. Quick, assessing, like she wasn't sure whether to be annoyed, amused, or intrigued.

Before I could stop myself, I was taking her in too. Her face was even better than I'd imagined. Pink, unvarnished lips, full and soft and dangerously kissable. A smattering of freckles dusted her cheeks and nose, giving her skin a kind of unfiltered glow. She looked to be about my age, maybe a little older, with eyes that... Damn, were they purple?

"Oh, shoot! I didn't see you there. Are you okay?" Southern charm dripped off her lips, warm and apologetic. She took a step back and adjusted her glasses. Small gold frames that made her look serious, intelligent, and sexy.

I stared for a second too long. "Uh, yeah. I'm good." I gave her a grin which I hoped wasn't too goofy, before sobering. "I hope that I didn't cause too much mess."

She tilted her head, studying me with her lips curling slightly at the edges before gesturing to the mess of pages spread around our feet. "Oh, this? This is fine. I'll have it all back together in a flash."

Before I could say I doubted it, she extended her hand, her smile warm and genuine. "I'm Mel, by the way."

I took her hand, a little too eagerly, feeling the slight heat in my cheeks.

"I'm Bobby," I said, my voice pitching embarrassingly high on the first syllable. I cleared my throat, trying to sound normal. Like I wasn't currently imagining what it'd be like to kiss her.

Mel smiled, her gaze flicking down to the mess of papers scattered across the floor. "Nice to meet you, Bobby," she said, her voice smooth but with a bit of a teasing edge. Could she read my mind?

Hoping she hadn't noticed my lack of composure, I said, "Let me help you with this mess."

She bit back a laugh, and I couldn't help but smile. She bent to gather the folders, her movements easy and graceful. "You're new to Marchfield Middle."

"How can you tell?" I knelt beside her, grabbing a few stray papers. "It's my first day. I was hoping to avoid embarrassing myself today."

Mel chuckled again, her eyes meeting mine, making my pulse skip. "It happens. We all have our... moments." She stood up, holding a stack of papers, and handed them to me. "Here, could you take these to my desk in the next room on the right? I'll get the rest."

I nodded, but my fingers brushed against hers, and an electric little jolt kickstarted my heart. Swallowing hard, I gripped the folders as if my life depended on it.

Walking out the door, I tried to focus on the task. But all I could think about was how her hand had felt against mine, the way she smelled like fresh citrus with a hint of spice.

The walls of her office were painted a soft cream. A few framed photos sat on the shelves and a bulletin board showcased colorful student artwork. A desk cluttered with papers and pens and two chairs took up most of the room, but the small touches on the walls caught my attention—the kind of things that made a place feel more personal.

A picture of a golden retriever, fur shining in the sunlight as it sprawled out in the grass, tongue lolling in what I assumed was bliss. Beside it, there was a family photo. Mel stood with an older couple, two kids dancing around them as they laughed together in a park, happy and normal.

For a brief moment, my chest tightened, sharp and unexpected, as memories washed through me. Family dinners, laughter in the kitchen, feeling like I belonged—all that ended when I came out.

The space between my family and me didn't just widen; it fractured clean and irreversible, like glass under pressure. Mom and Dad never yelled, never kicked me out. They just... stopped looking at me. One moment I was part of a family, and the next, I was a stranger eating dinner in the same house with ghosts.

When I couldn't fix it, I packed my bags, signed the papers, and joined the military.

After Afghanistan, I tried again. Maybe it was the brush with mortality or the long nights when silence pressed too hard on the edges of my mind. A call here, a message there—testing the waters, hoping time had softened them. But every attempt was met with brittle politeness, the kind that makes your chest ache more than anger ever could.

So, I stopped. And then, I buried it—like so many other things I didn't have the tools to fix.

I'd always been loud and cheerful, but after everything, I turned it up like a volume knob stuck on high. I smiled wider, laughed quicker, cracked jokes like it was my job. I became the one who never let things get too heavy.

But it was a mask, and I knew it. Underneath the bright façade was an ache I couldn't shake. A quiet, relentless craving for connection—for home, in whatever form that meant.

That's what brought me to Marchfield. A fresh start and a shot at building a different kind of family. And yet, I worried if it was all a cooked up fantasy. Could anyone love all the parts of me that I spent years hiding?

Mel's office felt foreign to me. It belonged to someone who knew exactly who she was and never once felt the need to apologize for it. The framed photos, the bold colors, even the way the chair was angled—all of it said this is my space.

My world was the opposite. It was shaped on shifting ground of glances and tone changes and the constant warning to be careful. I learned to read a room before I ever stepped inside it, to adapt before I even knew who I was adapting for. I was fluent in survival, but not in stillness.

And yet, something about her space—her presence—made me wonder. Maybe if I stood still long enough, I could learn what it felt like to be rooted. To take up space without flinching.

Mel swept in with the rest of the messy files in her arms, her movements efficient but unhurried. With a quiet confidence, she set them on the desk and nodded for me to do the same, as if this moment, this task, belonged to both of us.

"How long have you worked here?" I asked.

"I moved here last year," she said, straightening the files. "I'm the guidance director." She raised an eyebrow, her lips curling into a small smile. "You're the new science teacher, right?"

"Yeah, it's my first year teaching. I was in the Army before." I shrugged, trying to downplay it, but I could feel her studying me, her gaze more intense than before.

She nodded, her expression softening. "That's brave. I can't imagine the transition from the military to teaching. It must be a big adjustment."

I laughed, but it was a little self-deprecating. "Yeah, I'm still figuring it out. I'm used to structure and order, but this... this is different." I gestured vaguely to the cluttered office, though I couldn't help but admire how organized she seemed, even amid the mess. "But I'm excited."

"I can tell." She smiled, and the warmth in her expression made my heart stutter again. "I think you'll do just fine."

For a moment, neither of us spoke. The silence stretched between us, pulsing with something unspoken. The whole world narrowed to just us, the air charging with electricity, like the hush before a summer storm. Could she feel it too?

"So," I asked, trying to keep my voice steady, "what brought you to Marchfield?"

"After my husband..." Her smile faltered before she shrugged and gave me a small, almost reluctant smile. "I needed a fresh start. A new town, a new job."

Husband. The word rang in my ears.

Mel was straight.

"Sounds like you're exactly where you're meant to be," I said, smiling stiffly.

Her smile grew, just a little, but it was enough to make my chest tighten.

"Thanks, Bobby. That means a lot." She paused, her gaze holding mine a little longer than necessary. Those violet eyes sparkled with an emotion I couldn't decipher. Then, as quickly as it had come, the moment passed.

"Alright," I said, breaking the tension with a nervous laugh, my hands still fidgeting at my sides. "I should probably go get a key to my classroom."

Mel chuckled, the sound like music that floated through the room. Her lips quirked up at the corners, and I couldn't help but be drawn to the way her smile lit up her face. "Oh, Marsha should be back from the bank soon."

"Marsha. Great!" I was talking too fast, too loud. I cleared my throat, trying to tone it down. "She's the, uh..."

"She's our book and key keeper." Mel pointed to the left. "Her office is two doors down."

"Oh, gotcha." I shuffled my feet, not wanting to leave Mel's office. "Can I help you with those files?"

Her eyes flicked to the stack, papers sticking out in every which way. "Absolutely not. These are confidential. But if you need help with anything else, I'm always around. Just... don't sneak up on me again."

"Deal," I said. "Next time I'll bring a marching band and a fog machine."

With one last smile and a wave, I turned to leave, my pulse pounding wildly in my chest like I'd just sprinted a mile. I practically stumbled out of the office, the sound of my footsteps echoing down the hall, only to stop dead in my tracks when I remembered—I still needed a key to my classroom.

I cursed under my breath, a mix of frustration and embarrassment washing over me as I retraced my steps, hoping Mel didn't see me slink back into the office to find Marsha.

Chapter 2 Mel

M^el Leaning against the kitchen counter, I cradled my coffee in both hands, letting the warmth seep into my fingers. The early morning light filtered through the blinds, casting long horizontal shadows across the floor. It had been a year since I packed up and left Roanoke, and even now, the silence still felt strange. Peaceful, yes, but also unfamiliar.

Austin had never liked silence that stretched longer than a few seconds. Ten seconds in, and his knee would start to bounce. Fifteen, and he'd start complaining.

I shut my eyes and took a slow sip, forcing myself to focus on the present. Today was the first day of school. No baggage, no regrets. Just my job, my students, and a chance to make a difference.

Opening my eyes, I scanned the apartment. It was smaller than the house I'd shared with Austin, but that had been the point. Cozy, manageable. Mine. The open-concept living room and kitchen were lined with bookshelves crammed with novels, cookbooks I barely used, and framed photos of my parents and my dog, Moose.

He lay on the gray couch, sprawled out like he owned the place. The mixed-breed golden retriever with soulful brown eyes and a coat the color of toasted marshmallows had claimed the best spot in the apartment from day one. His fluffy tail thumped as I sank down beside him and scratched his floppy ears.

"Comfy?" I murmured.

His only answer was a heavy sigh before he stretched, rolling onto his back with his paws in the air—utterly at ease in a way I wasn't sure I'd ever be.

My phone buzzed on the coffee table.

Mom.

I sighed, knowing exactly how this conversation would go. "Hey, Mom."

"Sweetheart! Are you ready for the first day?"

I smiled despite myself. "It's only seven. I'm still at home drinking coffee."

"You need to eat something before you go. You always skip breakfast when you're nervous."

I rolled my eyes. "I'm not nervous."

"Liar," she teased. "How are you really?"

Mom didn't say anything right away, but I could hear her moving around, probably wiping down her spotless kitchen for the third time this morning, the rhythm of her cleaning almost like a subtle interrogation.

"You know," I said, trying to dodge the inevitable, "the real question is, how many times does one need to scrub the same counter before it reaches perfectly clean?"

"Depends," she answered with a teasing edge in her voice. "Are we talking about the counter or your life?"

I snorted, setting my mug down. "Ouch. Well, you're right about one thing: they both need a little more work."

There was a pause, and I could almost feel her smile through the phone. "Have you met anyone yet?"

"Mom," I complained even as my mind flashed to Bobby. Her bright smile and the way she radiated energy when she laughed. Had Austin ever looked at me with eyes that sparkly?

How would Mom would react? I'd never actually talked to her about the possibility of dating a woman, never said the words out loud.

Sure, I hadn't exactly hidden the fact that I was bi, but I hadn't exactly brought it up in conversation either. After all, I'd been in a heterosexual relationship, and that had been the norm for so long.

My pulse thundered in my ears. Taking a deep breath, I blurted it out. "I met a woman."

There was a heartbeat of silence. Then I heard it—the gentle clink of her mug being set down on the counter. Not rushed. Not dropped, but intentional. Like she wanted me to know she was really listening now.

"Oh?" Her voice was light, teasing, and completely unfazed. "Tell me more."

I let out a slow breath, forcing myself to relax. "Her name is Bobby. She's a new science teacher." A very attractive coworker who had made my stomach flip with a single handshake.

"What's she look like?" Mom asked, like she was asking about the weather—but I knew better.

I hesitated, frowning into the receiver. Why had I brought this up?

"She's, uh... she's got short brown hair," I started, keeping my tone light, casual. "Kind of military-cut, but not too severe."

Just long enough to thread my fingers through, if I ever got the chance.

"She's tall," I added. "Strong. Athletic." What would feel like to be pulled in close by her, held there, steady and safe?

"She's got this tan—like she's lived outside more than in. And she has sharp brown eyes." The kind that cut straight through me but didn't. Somehow, they softened when she looked at me.

There was a pause on the line, then, "How did you meet?"

I exhaled. "She crashed into me in the office and sent papers flying everywhere—pretty bad for first impression."

Mom laughed. "Sounds like an interesting meet cute."

"It wasn't a meet cute, Mom," I murmured, rubbing my thumb against the ceramic of my mug. I could practically hear her smirking through the phone.

"You know, honey," Mom said gently, "love is love. You don't have to explain it to me."

"Mom," I groaned, pressing a hand to my forehead.

"What?" she said, unapologetic. I could hear a cabinet door shut in the background. "Austin was an asshole, sweetheart. You deserve to be happy."

I swallowed, gripping the phone tighter. "I am happy," I said, too quickly. Too forcefully.

She sighed. "Melody."

The way she said my name, gentle and patient, made my chest tighten. She didn't need to say anything else. We'd had this conversation before many times.

"I just don't want you to keep punishing yourself," she said softly. "Austin made his choices, Mel. None of that was your fault."

My throat tightened. "I know," I lied. Because I did know. But knowing and believing were two very different things.

The truth was, I had spent years trying to be the perfect wife. The good wife. I had done everything right, and still, it had never been enough. Austin had always wanted more—more love, more passion, more of me than I could give. And when I hadn't been enough, he'd found someone else.

And died of a massive heart attack fucking her in our bed.

Anger had been the easiest thing to hold onto. Betrayal, too. But grief? That was trickier. Because how do you grieve someone who'd broken your heart? Someone who'd looked you in the eye, promised you the world, then tore it all to pieces? I wasn't sure I'd ever answer that question.

"I just think," Mom continued, carefully, "if you like Bobby, you should explore it."

"Mom," I said my face flushing hot. "I really have to get to work."

"Fine, fine," she said "But, Mel, try to be open, okay?"

"Talk to you later, Mom."

"Love you, sweetheart."

"Love you too."

I ended the call and set my phone down with a sigh.

Be open.

Finishing my coffee in one long sip, I pushed aside thoughts of Bobby's deep brown eyes, and how she'd breezed into town with her bright laugh. And I couldn't help but wonder why she'd chosen Marchfield of all places.

Because I hadn't moved all the way from Roanoke to find romance. I came to find myself. To remember how to be independent and strong in a place where people didn't know my whole story. A new town where I could rebuild without pitying looks and disappointed sighs.

I'd been here long enough to unpack the boxes, plant a small garden, and learn the names of the baristas at Pat's Bakery. But not long enough to forget the heartache that had chased me here. Not long enough to trust someone new.

With a deep breath, I gave Moose a final pat, grabbed my bag, and headed for the door.

It was time to start the school year.

BY LUNCH, I WAS STRETCHED thin.

Sitting in the teacher's cafeteria with a half-eaten salad in front of me, I let my mind drift back over the morning.

Helping students navigate their schedules was always a mix of problem-solving and patience. Some kids simply needed a room number, others required a pep talk, and then there were the ones whose anxiety sat just beneath the surface, coiled tight and ready to snap.

Like Claire.

She'd come into my office clutching her schedule like it was a life-line, her knuckles white, her lower lip bitten raw. "Ms. Brannaghan, I—I can't be in Mr. Morgan's Earth Science class. I can't."

Gesturing to the chair across from my desk, I kept my voice light. "Okay, let's talk about it."

It took some gentle prodding, but eventually, the words spilled out—her best friend wasn't in the class, she'd heard rumors about Bob Morgan being strict, and the idea of walking into a room full of strangers filled her with dread.

I understood that. Too well.

When Claire left, I promised to check in with her in one week, and she'd give the class a try.

Hurrying out of my office, I waved to Rhonda, the principal's administrative assistant. "I'm heading to lunch. Be back in twenty."

"Take thirty. You've been at it all morning."

The teachers' cafeteria was tucked behind the main lunchroom. A windowless, slightly fluorescent-lit room that smelled of burnt coffee and microwaved fish. The beige walls, mismatched chairs and tables, spoke of sadness and lost dreams, but I didn't mind. It was quiet and deserted. I wiped off a table, and was halfway through peeling the lid off my salad when the door swung open.

I didn't even have to look up to know who it was. The air shifted, and the faint scent of something clean and sun-warmed drifted in. My stomach did that stupid thing again, a little flip like it was glad before the rest of me had a say.

Bobby.

I stabbed a cherry tomato with more force than necessary, heat creeping up my neck as my body reacted to her. It had been a long time since I'd felt anything this sudden. And I wasn't sure I liked it.

"Whoa, is this where the cool kids eat?" Bobby's voice rang out, full of playful mock horror. "Why do I feel like I should've packed a Lunchable?"

Snorting despite myself, I glanced up as she dropped into the chair across from me, setting down a cafeteria tray with what could generously be called food. She wrinkled her nose at the suspiciously grayish chicken sandwich.

"I wouldn't," I warned, nodding toward it. "Unless you've got a strong stomach."

"Army," Bobby said with a wink, tearing open a packet of mayo. "I've eaten worse."

She squeezed the condiment onto the sandwich, my brain still catching up to the casual way she mentioned her past as I pieced things together. There was more to her than just an easy smile and bright brown eyes. She was new to teaching. She was in her thirties. She had served.

"How's your day been so far?" I asked, leaning forward, eager to get her perspective.

Bobby grinned, a little rueful. "Well, I'm pretty sure my first block thinks I'm a walking science experiment."

I couldn't help but laugh. "On my first day in Roanoke, I passed out when a student picked a tick off themselves in the middle of class and started bleeding. It wasn't long after that I started my coursework for guidance."

Her eyebrows shot up, and I could see a flash of concern in her brown eyes. Despite myself, I wondered how her lips would look if she were focused on me instead of trying not to choke on her coffee.

"Do you have that reaction every time you see blood?"

Shaking the thoughts out of my head, I tried not to look like a deer caught in headlights. "No," I replied, forcing a laugh. "I just have a deep psychological aversion to ticks."

"Fair enough," Bobby nodded. "I don't like those creepy bloodsuckers either. Thankfully nothing so dramatic happened in my class today. It was mostly just me trying not to cry when I couldn't get the screen to work. One kid tried to help, but then he broke the remote, and the kids spent half the lesson watching me panic."

Suppressing a chuckle, I said, "Sounds like a solid start..."

She shrugged, and my laughter dried up as I noticed how her muscles shifted under the fabric of her shirt. The subtle flex of her shoulders and how her biceps moved with a kind of effortless grace had me doing a double-take. Her shirt clung just enough to show off the strength in her frame. The urge to reach out and run my hand across her shoulder and down her arm made my palm tingle.

Swallowing hard, I quickly looked away, trying to calm the sudden rush of heat in my chest. Damn, Bobby had a way of making me lose track of what I was saying. "There's... um, nothing quite like technical failure to make you feel like you've lost all control."

Bobby's lips twitched with amusement. "Exactly. And by the time lunch came around, I was questioning my entire life's decisions." She met my eyes, and I felt the weight of her gaze all the way to my toes. "Until I saw you."

The comment caught me off guard, and for a moment, I felt my face turn beet red. I quickly looked away, pretending to focus on putting my salad into my lunch bag, but her words echoed in my head, sent my heart into overdrive.

"Lucky for you, you survived. And you got to sit with me at the cool kids' table. So, winning all around," I said, trying to brush off the warmth spreading through me.

Bobby raised her water bottle like a trophy, her eyes sparkling with something playful, almost daring. "I'm considering it my victory lap," she said with a smirk that squeezed my heart.

"I'll be sure to save a seat for you tomorrow, then," I said, my voice betraying the slight breathlessness I couldn't hide.

Her smile was slow, a little more knowing this time. And as the bell rang, signaling the end of lunch, I felt an odd longing as she stood and grabbed her empty tray. I watched her walk away, and despite knowing this was a problem, I was already looking forward to the next time we'd meet.

Chapter 3

Bobby

At the end of the day, I surveyed the wreckage of my classroom. Chairs sat at odd angles. A stack of papers fanned across my desk and onto the floor like a hurricane had torn through. My whiteboard was covered in the half-erased diagram of a flower, and the words *Tiff wuz Here.*

Did I even have a Tiff in my classes?

I shrugged. I'd survived my first day. And I'd been through worse. A hell of a lot worse.

I exhaled slowly, rolling the stiffness from my shoulders. My body still carried the muscle memory of hauling gear in the punishing heat of Afghanistan, of moving through training drills that pushed me to the edge of exhaustion. The Army had toughened me, sharpened me into something unbreakable. And yet, I'd walked into this classroom and nearly been taken out by a faulty projector screen and a pack of seventh graders with too many questions.

Oz would've had a field day with that.

Thinking of him made me smile. We'd met in the middle of the worst of it. Two wide-eyed soldiers in a place with no forgiveness. He'd watched my back, and I'd cracked jokes when things got too heavy.

Oz had slipped into teaching in New York like it was second nature while I stood amidst the ruins of my first day, wondering if I'd made a terrible mistake.

I needed a friend. Someone who didn't ask too many questions, who didn't care about every little detail about my tragic past. Who could hang out and offer a sliver of the comfort I'd left behind. They didn't need to see past my sarcasm and the fake grin, just help make Marchfield feel more like home.

A knock at my open door pulled me from my thoughts.

Keith Payt leaned against the doorframe. The special education teacher had the easy confidence of someone been around the block a few times. Tall, broad-shouldered but not bulky, with a head of perpetually messy brown hair and a beard. He came off as a flirt—perpetually amused, a little shallow.

Word in the teacher's lounge was that he had a reputation for sleeping around. I'd met a lot of guys like that in the Army, and at first, I believed it. He didn't take things too seriously, but he had a calm energy that I liked. But there was something about him I couldn't quite put my finger on. His smile faded when the conversation veered into anything personal, like there was a part of him he didn't want anyone to see. It made me wonder if he wasn't as carefree as he seemed.

"You still standing?" he asked, his voice light and teasing.

"Barely," I admitted, gesturing to the mess around me. "Is it always this bad?"

Keith snorted, stepping inside. "First day's always rough. Kids are testing you, seeing what they can get away with." He scanned the room, then grinned. "Judging by the state of things, I'd say they gave you a proper initiation."

I groaned, dragging a hand down my face. "Good to know my suffering is part of a long-standing tradition."

"Hey, at least you didn't cry in the supply closet. That's a win in my book."

I raised an eyebrow. "Is that... something you did?"

Keith smirked. "No, but I've seen it happen. New teachers should never underestimate middle schoolers. They're agents of chaos."

"No argument there." I exhaled, shaking my head. "I swear, I've been through military training less stressful than today."

Keith let out a low chuckle. "Yeah, well, they don't follow a chain of command."

Slouching into a student chair, I let my head fall back. "Why did no one warn me?"

"Oh, I'm sure you were warned," he said, propping himself against my desk. "You just couldn't believe it. But since I'm feeling generous, I'll give you the Marchfield Survival Guide—patent pending."

Crossing my arms over my chest, I asked, "Do I need to take notes?"

"Nah," he said with a smirk. "Alright, rule one: Avoid the copier in the eighth-grade hall. That thing is older than sin, and if you so much as breathe near it, it'll jam. And guess what? If you're the last person to touch it, it's your problem."

I groaned. "That explains why I saw Marnie McQuistion swearing at it during lunch."

Keith nodded solemnly. "She's been at war with that thing for a decade. Moving on—rule two: Never let the kids see you cry. They smell weakness, and if they do? You're done for."

"Please," I scoffed, "I don't cry."

Keith's grin widened. "Uh-huh. Talk to me again after parent conferences."

I frowned but didn't argue.

"And the most important rule," he said, leaning in conspiratorially, "if you like someone, don't be subtle. Marchfield thrives on gossip. Make eye contact with someone for more than three seconds? The rumormongers will say you're engaged. Sit next to them at lunch? They'll expect a wedding registry by Friday."

"So, what you're saying is people are already gossiping about Mel and me?"

Keith let out a low laugh. "Oh, girl. The mill is grinding."

I hesitated. "What should I do? Stay away from her?"

"Well, my philosophy has always been to give them a show." Keith stretched his arms over his head. "I had a very enthusiastic date with the French teacher last year, and by the time I walked in the next morning, half the staff thought we were ready to pick out baby names."

"And you were okay with that?" I snorted.

He shrugged. "Why fight it?" Then he shot me a knowing grin. "But you should keep it in mind unless you want to be the next hot topic."

I exhaled slowly, my mind drifting back to my conversations with Mel, which was ridiculous because she was straight.

Not that it mattered.

Even if she weren't, I had enough to worry about without adding faculty gossip to the list.

Still, I caught myself smiling, just a little, before shaking my head and reaching for my laptop. "Considering my love life is nonexistent, I think I'm safe."

Keith tapped his fingers against the doorway. "Give it time, new girl. Give it time." Then, with a wink, he sauntered out the door, whistling as he went.

SOMEHOW I MANAGED TO slog through the rest of the week, and when the last bell rang, I grabbed my bag, feeling like I was dragging a mountain behind me. As I stepped out of the building, the warm, humid Virginia air hit me like a wet towel, and I sucked in a deep breath. The first week was done.

Dragging myself toward my Jeep, I counted down the seconds before I could collapse on my couch with a beer and finally give my brain a break. But as I rounded the corner, I spotted Mel walking ahead of me.

My steps slowed instinctively, my attention snapping to her like a magnet.

Her movements were fluid and sure, like she had the world figured out. She wore a simple navy blouse, the sleeves rolled neatly to her elbows, paired with tailored white pants. Even her sneakers, clean and bright, felt less like practicality and more like the final brushstroke on a painting.

Soft waves of blonde-brown hair fell around her shoulders, bouncing with each step. Next to her, I looked like a clumsy mess.

Why was I so thrown by her presence? We'd only spoken a handful of times, and yet there was something magnetic about her. I let out a breath, unsure if I should call out to her or just let her go.

She turned as if she'd heard me. Her violet eyes met mine, and that was it. I had no idea what was happening, but I couldn't help walking toward her.

Grinning like an idiot, I tried to keep my composure. "Hey, Mel," I called, giving her what I hoped was a casual wave.

She raised an eyebrow, a small smile tugging at the corner of her lips. "Bobby. Hi."

"Hi. I was just heading home." I shrugged, leaning against my Jeep. Doing my best to appear cool and collected, I let my school bag slide with a thud onto the pavement. "I have to say, I'm a little envious of the way you walk out of this place every day. No stress, no sweat."

Mel raised an eyebrow. "That sounds heavy."

I glanced down at the bag, then back up at her. "Only emotionally."

She chuckled. "You're assuming I have no stress. I'd argue guidance has a different kind of stress."

"Right, yeah. Totally," I said, words tumbling out before I could catch them. "I don't know what I'm talking about—I've been here, what, five minutes?"

I laughed, a little too loudly, gave a little finger-gun salute, then added, "But hey, I'm just here to bring the sunshine."

Cool. Real smooth.

She tilted her head, a teasing glint in her eye. "Are you always this upbeat, or is it just for me?"

"Hey, what can I say? You can't sweat the small stuff." I winked, hoping it covered the anxiety bubbling inside me.

Her smile deepened, but she raised an eyebrow. "You sure you're not hiding a darker side?"

I could feel my heart pounding in my chest, like it was trying to escape. I leaned in just a little, my voice dropping low as I gave her the words I carried but barely let anyone hear.

"I've got a few secrets." I leaned in just a little, lowering my voice. "I'm queer."

The words slipped out before I could stop them—too fast, too exposed. Why was I telling Mel this now? We weren't even talking about anything personal. It wasn't planned, it wasn't polished. But maybe that was the point.

Something about Mel made me believe there was a sliver of hope that I could have a family of my own one day. Not the kind that was blood-bound and tied to old hurts, but a new one. A chosen family, one built on trust, understanding, and acceptance.

I was tired of tiptoeing, of gauging the temperature of a room before deciding whether or not to be myself. And I couldn't take it back now. All I could do was wait and see how she'd react, my heart hammering behind a suddenly too-tight smile.

She blinked. Cocked her head at me and said, "Oh. Okay."

Okay?

I had to fight the urge to laugh, but because this was going so well, I couldn't stop the next words from tumbling out of my mouth. "What about you? You're straight, right?"

Her lips quirked up into a half-smile, her eyes locking onto mine as she took a step closer. "Not exactly."

My heart skipped a beat, and the air between us shifted, the tension building. "Not exactly? What does that mean?"

She sighed softly, glancing away briefly before meeting my gaze again. "Look, Bobby... I'm bi. But I still have things to figure out."

My breath caught, just for a second, like my heart had stepped forward before the rest of me could catch up. I'd braced for polite rejection, the kind that stings even when it's gentle. But instead, there was this... opening.

Still, the words *I still have things to figure out* hung between us. I knew that terrain—shifting, complicated. I'd lived in it for years and made peace with most of it.

So, I nodded, trying to keep my voice light even as my chest thudded. "Yeah. That makes two of us, and hey, if you ever want some company with no strings. Just... you know, two people still figuring things out."

She blinked at me, her eyes shifting, like she was sizing up my intentions.

I tried not to hold my breath, but my mind was already racing. Part of me wanted to make a joke, but the rest of me was just... curious.

Mel studied me for a moment, her expression unreadable before she gave me a half-smile and took a step back. "Maybe."

I shrugged, pretending to be unaffected, though my mind was already plowing toward the next step. I hadn't expected this conversation turn out this way, but I wasn't about to overthink it.

"Fair enough," I said, raising an eyebrow with a grin. "Guess I'll just have to keep asking until you figure it out."

She shook her head before moving toward her car. "Good night, Bobby."

A small thrill ran through me as I watched her drive away.

She hadn't said no, and that was enough for now.

Chapter 4

Mel Marchfield's first meeting of the Student Council Association was always a bit crazy, but that was to be expected. A cafeteria filled with a hundred middle schoolers eager to change the dress code or cafeteria menu meant I had to balance enthusiasm with structure.

We'd just finished playing The Tallest Tower, a team-based game where students worked together using marshmallows and uncooked spaghetti to construct the tallest free-standing structure. It had been a great icebreaker, especially when the towers inevitably collapsed at the last second, sending marshmallows flying and students into fits of laughter.

The mix of sixth, seventh, and eighth graders had worked surprisingly well together. Henry, a meticulous eighth-grader, had taken charge of one of the groups' bases, while Zoe, a chatty seventh-grader, added wild additions. Their tower measured over two feet tall before it wobbled and crumbled, making them the undisputed winners.

"Okay, settle down," I called over the chatter, clapping my hands twice. It took a moment, but eventually, the students echoed my clap and the volume lowered.

The students moved to sit at the long lunch tables with attached seats, their voices bouncing off the tiled floor and high ceilings. The scent of sanitizer and stale chicken nuggets hung in the air. Some students leaned forward eagerly, while others slouched, arms crossed, sizing up their peers.

"We've got a busy year ahead of us, starting with next week's County-Wide Meeting with student councils from all the middle schools in the area." I picked up the stack of permission slips from the table. "I need each of you to take one of these home and get it signed and return it to me by the end of the week."

As I passed out the papers, I continued, "We also need a couple of parent chaperones. If your parent or guardian can come with us, please let me know."

Silence.

Not a single hand went up. A few students suddenly found their shoelaces very interesting, while others glanced around, hoping someone else would volunteer first.

I sighed. "Really? No one?"

A few students shook their heads. One brave seventh-grader, Max, spoke up. "My mom is busy with work."

"Mine too," added Sophie.

"My dad has to watch my little brothers," another student chimed in.

A chorus of similar responses followed. I resisted the urge to groan. Middle schoolers were independent enough to want these experiences but still young enough to need adults to keep an eye on them.

I'd already asked quite a few faculty members, but everyone had turned me down. I'd caught up with Keith right before the meeting in the copy room, where he was locked in a battle with the ancient, temperamental copier.

"Hey," I said, leaning against the doorway. "You busy next Thursday?"

He didn't even glance up. "Is that a trick question?"

"Field trip," I said, holding up the clipboard. "SCA's going to the City-Wide meeting, and I need chaperones."

Keith let out a dramatic groan, then banged the side of the copier like he was trying to summon a demon. "God, I'd love to say yes, but

I've got an IEP meeting marathon that day. Five in a row. I won't even get a lunch. Sorry, Mel."

I sighed. "Worth a shot."

As I turned to go, I spotted Marnie passing with a bag of groceries for her teen living class tucked under her arm.

I quickened my pace to catch up. "Any chance you're free next Thursday? SCA field trip. I'm desperate."

She gave me a sympathetic look. "Ugh, I wish. But I've got a curriculum pacing meeting that afternoon with the district. They're rolling out changes for next semester, and if I miss it, I'll be flying blind. I'd totally help otherwise." I nodded, trying not to let the disappointment show.

"No worries. I'll keep asking."

"Good luck." She winced. "You'll need it."

Now as the meeting wrapped up, I tried to think of another adult I could invite on the trip, but I came up empty.

As I followed the students out of the cafeteria and into the main hall, the noise tripled. Laughter, questions, and over-the-top stories echoed off the walls in a tidal wave of teenage energy.

"Ms. Brannaghan, do we get extra credit for being on SCA?" A tiny girl with pretty braids danced around me with a bright smile.

Forcing a smile, I said, "Sorry, Samyah. But you do get the satisfaction of making a difference in our school."

Her friend, a tall, thin girl with long hair extensions, chimed in, "Can we petition to replace all the water fountains with soda machines?"

"I'm not sure that's the biggest issue students face at Marchfield."

Ahead of us, a group of sixth-graders in matching red basketball jerseys whispered conspiratorially. One turned back and asked, "Is it true the eighth graders get free candy and soda on Fridays?"

I laughed. "I wish. If that were true, I'd bum some from Mr. Becken."

Outside, the students piled onto the buses, still chattering and tossing ideas back and forth. I waved as the doors closed, shaking my head as Tim Mueller pulled down the window and called, "Can we get a school pet? Maybe a llama?"

As the last bus rumbled out of the parking lot, I took a deep breath, enjoying the sudden quiet. The cool evening air carried the faint scent of cut grass and asphalt, a welcome contrast to the cafeteria's overwhelming mix of disinfectant and mystery meat.

Relaxing, I inhaled deeply, letting the late afternoon air settle my nerves. The new SCA wasn't just another responsibility—it was part of my fresh start. Each student I connected with reminded me that I didn't have to be flawless to matter. I could show up, mess up, and still be enough. Here in Marchfield, maybe for the first time in a long while, I felt like I could just be me.

Reviewing my mental my to-do list, I added email parents about volunteers to stop by the grocery for dog food and figure out what to have for dinner.

Taking one more deep breath, I tried to convince myself to head back inside the school.

"Hey." A voice sliced through the air, sharp and unexpected, just inches from my ear.

Spinning around, I yelped as I nearly launched myself headfirst into a nearby bush. My dress pumps wobbled beneath me, a heel catching on the uneven sidewalk, sending me into a wild stagger. My arms flailed out in a desperate windmill. My heart jumped into my throat before I managed to regain my balance.

"Damn it, Bobby!" I clutched my chest. "Are you trying to give me a heart attack?"

She shrugged, not looking the least bit sorry. "You need to work on your survival reaction."

I narrowed my eyes, jerking away. Her blue cotton button-down shirt clung to her curves. Her eyes locked onto mine, and I had to force myself not to look too long. That grin of hers, playful and confident, stirred something inside me that I definitely wasn't ready to feel. It irritated me more than I cared to admit.

"I'll add develop ninja-like reflexes to my never-ending list."

She chuckled. "So, how'd the meeting go? Any power-hungry middle schoolers trying to overthrow the system?"

"Give them time." I exhaled, shaking my head. "Right now, they're too focused on installing soda machines and getting an emotional support llama."

"Ah, classic." She nodded solemnly, but her eyes flashed with mischief.

"Were you lurking out here just to scare me, or do you need something?"

"Bit of both," she admitted.

I huffed a laugh. "Okay."

She gave me a once-over, tilting her head. "You look exhausted."

"You are full of compliments today."

"I mean it in the nicest way."

"Sure," I said, waving her off. "I need to go inside and beg some parents to chaperone the County-Wide SCA Meeting next week."

Bobby's brows lifted. "You're short?"

I snorted. "Try completely lacking. Not a single volunteer."

She rocked back on her heels. "I'll do it."

I blinked. "What?"

"I'll chaperone," she repeated, shrugging like it was the simplest thing in the world.

"Wait—no. I mean, thank you, but you really don't have to do that," she said quickly, already backpedaling. "You... don't want to spend an evening on a bus with a bunch of middle schoolers, sitting through a student council meeting and making sure no one gets lost or starts a prank war."

She shrugged. "Sounds like basic training. Sweet memories."

I hesitated. It wasn't that I didn't appreciate the help. God, I just needed a warm body, but letting her in, even just for a field trip, felt... bigger than it should. Like I was opening a door I'd kept shut for a reason.

"You sure?" I asked, arms crossed, trying to sound casual.

But Bobby didn't flinch. "I wouldn't have offered if I didn't mean it. I've got the time. Besides, hanging out with a bus full of middle schoolers sounds like a party."

I rolled my eyes. "You're out of your mind."

"Maybe," she said, grinning. "But I'm in."

And just like that, I had a chaperone.

"Don't say I didn't warn you."

Bobby grinned. "Oh, I'm counting on it."

I rolled my eyes. "Thanks for volunteering as tribute."

"And here I thought you'd at least offer me a bow and arrow," she shot back.

"Careful." I smirked. "Katniss was my gay awakening. You start slinging arrows and I might not survive the trip."

Was I flirting with Bobby? Like, actually flirting? My stomach flipped. I couldn't even remember the last time I'd flirted with anyone—had I ever? Of course, I probably flirted with Austin, but that was so long ago.

And now, apparently, I was doing it with a woman who could probably bench-press me. What was I thinking? I needed to stop. Pull it together. Be normal.

My brain scrambled for something to say to cover it, but nothing came, so I sputtered. "I just... you know, respect a good archery skill. Definitely not... uh... flirting. Totally not... Oh God, I'm shutting up now."

I pivoted toward the school building. I had work to do. I could ignore this strange pull and flicker of tension.

I was happy. Stable. I had friends, Moose, a rhythm to my life that finally felt like mine. I didn't need a relationship. What I needed was space to breathe, to be myself without the weight of anyone's expectations because what if I lost what little balance I'd carved out?

And yet... there was something about Bobby that unsettled me in the most inconvenient way. A warmth under my skin. A curiosity I didn't want. I wasn't looking for anything. I wasn't ready for anything. But that didn't stop the way my thoughts kept drifting back to her, even when I knew better.

Without hearing her move, I felt her presence behind me, the heat radiating from her, just inches away.

"Mel, I..."

She broke off, and I knew I should brush her off. Tell her to leave me alone. I needed to regain control. But I couldn't steady my breath. Every part of me screamed to stay calm, to regain some distance, but it was impossible when every nerve was strung tight, responding to her, drawn in by her.

Bobby's eyes were on me. The urge to glance over my shoulder and catch her smirk, which I both craved and resented, was almost impossible to resist.

Would she kiss me? The thought nearly stopped my heart. How would it feel to touch her, to let her touch me? It had been so long since I'd let anyone in, and the idea was both terrifying and exhilarating.

The air between us crackled with something unspoken, daring me to react.

I couldn't. I couldn't do this. Not now. I had too much to lose. I cherished order and serenity, and Bobby was too complicated and messy.

Without thinking, I spun, making a quick break for the door, my steps faster than I intended. Unlocking it with my badge, my fingers shook slightly as I shoved it open too forcefully, the sound of the metal against the frame ringing in the quiet.

"Good night," I muttered, my voice tight, not looking back as I fled into the school, my heart racing like it was trying to outrun my feelings.

Chapter 5

M^{el} I stared at my laptop screen, the cursor blinking in quiet accusation. The email I'd been trying to compose for the last ten minutes remained unfinished, half a sentence hanging there like my scattered thoughts.

Outside my office window, the sun had already begun its slow descent. Almost 6:00 PM, and I was still here, still pretending I was working. I rubbed at my temples, willing myself to focus, but my brain refused to cooperate, stubbornly stuck somewhere between a stack of paperwork, a full email box, and her.

It had been years since I was some love-struck teenager, yet here I was, flustered and distracted. Bobby was under my skin like an itch I couldn't scratch, but I'd learned my lesson about attraction. It burned out quickly and left nothing but heartbreak behind.

With a frustrated sigh, I leaned back, running a hand through my hair. Bobby was a coworker, and I had done the right thing by not engaging. Now, I just needed to shake it off.

The knock on my office door startled me, and I swiveled my chair toward it just as Audrey poked her head in.

"Hey, you busy?" Audrey asked, not waiting for an answer as she stepped inside with Val right behind her. Audrey's red hair caught the light, a striking contrast against her fair skin, while Val, tan as always, tossed her dark waves over her shoulder. Their bright smiles immediately put me on edge.

"Just finishing up," I said, even though I'd accomplished nothing. "What's up?"

"We're going for a drink," Val said, plopping down in the chair across from me. "You should come."

"Oh, I don't know—" I shook my head.

"Don't even start," Audrey cut in, crossing her arms. "You've been in here all evening. You need a break."

"I have things to—"

Val grinned. "Yeah, we get it, you're busy. But sometimes you need to hang out with your friends."

I opened my mouth to argue, then snapped it shut. Val was right. Friendships nurtured the soul. What was the point of making a fresh start if I wasn't going to embrace it?

Audrey tilted her head, watching me too closely. "And we want to know why you're so jumpy lately."

"Jumpy? I'm not jumpy," I said quickly, too quickly.

Their eyes narrowed in tandem, and I cursed under my breath.

"Mel," Val said, her voice dripping with suspicion. "Does it have anything to do with Bobby Nooney?"

Choking on air, I coughed as my face heated. "What? No! Why would—why would you even—"

Audrey's grin was downright devious. "Oh, this is definitely about Bobby."

"It is not!"

Val leaned forward, resting her chin on her hand. "I heard you two looked very cozy after the buses left today."

Dropping my head onto my desk, I groaned. "I hate both of you."

Audrey laughed. "You'll hate us less after a drink. Come on, Mel, you need a distraction."

Peeking at them, I knew I wasn't getting out of this. And maybe they were right. I did need a distraction.

With a sigh, I grabbed my bag. "Fine. But if you two start analyzing my life over cocktails, I'm leaving."

"No promises," Val said, grinning as she linked her arm through mine while Audrey nudged me toward the door.

Apparently, Thursday was the new Friday at Barrel. The low hum of conversation mingled with bursts of laughter was punctuated by the sharp thunk of axes striking targets at the back of the space. The scent of wood shavings and craft beer hung in the air, and every table seemed full of locals.

Audrey, Val, and I perched on tall chairs at a high-top table. The glow from the neon Michelob sign cast blue shadows on Audrey's fair skin. Val sipped at her cocktail, her dark eyes scanning the room. I wrapped my hands around my glass, hoping the cool condensation would somehow ground me.

"So," Audrey started, stretching out the word, "let's talk about Bobby."

"Let's not," I groaned.

Val smirked, drumming her fingers against her glass. "Oh, let's. Because you've been weird since she started working with us."

"No, I haven't," I muttered, sipping my drink. But even as I said it, I knew it wasn't true. I'd been distracted, restless, and hyper-aware every time Bobby entered a room. Usually, I was good at compartmentalizing, keeping people at arm's length, and yet, here I was, mentally cataloging every detail about the woman.

Audrey propped her elbow on the table, a smug smile tugging at her lips. "Then why are you blushing?"

Scowling at my glass, I sighed. "Because you two are pissing me off."

Val waved off my deflection. "So, are we pretending she's not hot? Because I feel like that's a disservice to her—and honestly, to anyone who's ever appreciated strong arms, cheekbones that could cut glass, and a walk that says I know exactly what I'm doing."

Maybe Val should date her. The random thought hit harder than I expected, sending a sharp pang of jealousy curling in my chest.

"I never said Bobby wasn't attractive," I said quickly, a little too defensively. "That's not the issue."

"Oh?" Audrey's eyebrows lifted. "And what is the issue, exactly?"

The fact that Bobby made me feel completely off-kilter with nothing more than a look? That my heart had no business speeding up whenever she was close?

There were simple, logical rules. Avoid entanglements. Love hurt. It left people broken and disappointed. I'd learned that lesson, but every time Bobby smiled at me, I felt a tiny fracture in the walls I'd built.

"She's just... Bobby." I waved a hand, as if that explained anything.

Val snorted. "That is the weakest excuse I've ever heard."

I narrowed my eyes at her. "Easy for you to say. You're single. You don't have any baggage, and you need to overthink every little feeling."

Audrey leaned forward, eyes sharp. "So, are you actually interested, or just freaked out because you could be?"

I tensed, gripping my glass a little too tightly. I hated that they could read me this well.

Before I could respond, a loud cheer erupted from the axe-throwing lanes. My head turned automatically, scanning past the pool tables until my gaze landed on Bobby. She stood with Keith and a few other people in front of a wooden target, her sleeves rolled up, showing off strong forearms. She was laughing, full of confidence, completely in her element.

A pretty blonde stepped closer, murmuring something in Bobby's ear. Whatever she said must've been funny because Bobby threw her head back, laughing in an uninhibited way that made my stomach tighten.

I took a too-large gulp of my drink, the burn doing nothing to dull the realization.

I was jealous.

There was no denying it. The thought of another woman with Bobby made my stomach twist in a way that was absolutely not casual. I crossed my arms, trying to play it off, but the heat was already rising in my face.

Bobby wasn't mine. She wasn't anyone's, and yet the image of that woman brushing a hand against Bobby's arm made my chest tighten like I'd swallowed a fist.

Val's eyes narrowed, tracking my gaze. "Oh, this is interesting."

I exhaled sharply. "It's nothing."

Audrey rested her chin on her palm, eyes narrowing like she was studying a lab sample. "You're jealous."

My head snapped toward her. "I am not."

She didn't even blink. "Please. You went rigid the second you saw that woman touch Bobby. You're practically vibrating."

Val leaned back in her chair, smug. "It's obvious."

I opened my mouth to argue, then closed it again, jaw tight. Damn it. Was I really that transparent?

"Bobby can date whomever she wants," I said, aiming for breezy but landing somewhere between defensive and delusional.

"Whomever. Wow," Audrey said, laughing. "Look at you, bringing grammar into your emotional repression."

Val snorted. "You're a nerd and a terrible liar."

I groaned, rubbing my temples. "I don't get jealous. I have Moose. I'm perfectly happy."

Audrey raised an eyebrow, her tone light but cutting. "Sweetie, Moose is a dog. You're not perfectly happy."

I closed my eyes briefly, willing away the mess of emotions clawing at my ribs. I'd had my fill tonight.

Audrey and Val exchanged a grin.

"Oh, Mel," Audrey said sympathetically. "You've caught feelings."

I scowled, wishing she were wrong but unable to deny it. "Gross."

Chapter 6

Bobby

I was not a subtle person. Never had been. Never would be.

I liked Mel and saw no point in sitting around and brooding about it. That wasn't my style. My style was direct, strategic action. And, if I was being honest, sometimes it bordered on ridiculous.

Mel was... complicated. She was sharp-witted, cool, and had this way of looking at me that made my brain short-circuit. She was also guarded, stubborn as hell, and resistant to romance. But there were moments when I thought she might want me.

Like when she laughed at something stupid I said and her eyes lit up. Or when she lingered after a conversation, her posture softening just enough to show she wasn't all business. And then there were the times her cheeks flushed, just a little, when she got too close.

It wasn't much, but it was there.

And I could work with that.

I tapped my fingers against my desk, thinking If I came on too strong, she'd run. If I played it too cool, she'd ignore me. I needed something in between that kept me on her radar without setting off all her internal alarms.

A slow burn workplace wooing.

I grinned. This would be fun.

Step one: infiltration. Work into her daily routine in a way that felt natural. Casual run-ins, conveniently timed walks to our cars, and shared duty posts. Subtle but consistent.

Step two: psychological warfare. I needed to throw her off balance. Fluster her.

Step three: humor.

I grabbed a notepad and scrawled out my first move.

One of your mentees just told me I'm their
favorite adult in the building.
Tough break, Counselor.

I folded the note, grinning.

The next day, I ended my first block two minutes early and bribed a group of eighth graders with Jolly Ranchers to deliver my note.

"Alright, team," I said, crouching down in front of my chosen group of messengers. "Your mission, should you choose to accept it, is to deliver this note to Ms. Brannaghan with the utmost secrecy and style. Extra candy if you can make her blush."

"Can we read it first?" Corben asked, eyes gleaming with mischief.

"Absolutely not," I said, handing over the folded paper. "The fate of this operation depends on discretion."

Corben nodded, her shoulders straightening. She nodded to Samantha and Quinn, and after a quick huddle, they scampered out the door like caffeinated squirrels.

Perfect.

I leaned back against my desk, crossing my arms as I imagined Mel's reaction. She'd roll her eyes. Maybe huff out an exasperated sigh. But if I was lucky, she'd smile.

And that was worth every bit of trouble I was about to get into.

WHEN I RETURNED TO my classroom after lunch, I found her answer.

A single sticky note, slapped onto my whiteboard in Mel's no-nonsense handwriting.

Enjoy it while it lasts.

I have the power to change schedules.

I grinned. Game on.

The next morning, I arrived early enough to leave a rose along with this poem on her desk:

Roses are red,
Violets are blue,
This school would be boring,
If it weren't for you

When she didn't respond, I sent another message via Corben's courier service. A small jar filled with marbles, complete with a note:

Heard you lost these.

No response.

Maybe I'd pushed her too far.

But later, when I walked into the cafeteria at lunch, she pounced. Grabbing my wrist with surprising urgency, she yanked me toward the dimly lit supply closet tucked beside the cafeteria entrance. The air inside smelled faintly of cleaning supplies and paper, and shelves lined with boxes were on all sides.

Her dark blazer was crisp, the white blouse tucked in perfectly, like she had her entire life together. If it weren't for the determined set of her jaw and the way her purple eyes darkened to almost black with intensity, I might've believed she was as cool as a cucumber.

Her grip didn't loosen. If anything, it tightened—like whatever she had to say couldn't wait another second. Turning her sharp gaze on me, she held up the jar of marbles. "This has gone too far."

I shrugged, shoving my hands in my pockets. "Define too far."

Her eyes narrowed. "You're using children as your personal delivery service."

"Correction." I held up a finger. "I'm using volunteers."

She made a strangled sound, a noise between exasperation and disbelief. Her lips parted as if to laugh before pressing into a tight line. I swore I saw the faintest tinge of pink creeping up her neck, blooming over her collarbone and disappearing beneath the crisp neckline of her blouse.

Mel took a slow, deep breath as if mentally counting to ten. "People think you like me."

I smirked. "Oh? What are they saying? That we're a picture-perfect couple? That our chemistry is off the charts? That you can't resist my charm?"

Mel leveled me with a look. "Oh my God! I'm going to strangle you with my lanyard."

I chuckled. "Kinky. But I'd prefer we went on a date first."

Mel groaned, pressing her fingers to her temples. "I walked right into that."

"You really did," I agreed, grinning. "So, what exactly are people saying?"

Mel hesitated. Her delicate fingers fisting at her sides.

"Ohhh." I leaned in. "Maybe you like that they're talking."

Mel's face was unreadable, but the pink creeping up her neck gave her away. "Wrong. I wish everyone, including you, would shut up."

"And yet, you dragged me in here." Bobby wiggled her eyebrows. "Almost like you want them to talk."

"You are the most aggravating person I have ever met."

I grinned. "That can't possibly be true. You work in a middle school."

She narrowed her eyes. "Exactly. And yet, you have somehow surpassed every smart-mouthed teen I've ever dealt with."

I pressed a hand to my chest, feigning offense. "Wow. That's impressive even for me. Thank you."

"It wasn't a compliment."

"Didn't sound like an insult either."

She exhaled sharply, dragging a hand through her hair, which mussed it enough to make my brain short-circuit for a second. "You cannot use students as your personal matchmaking service."

"Why not? They seem to be doing a great job."

"They're twelve."

I shrugged. "Kids are perceptive. They see the tension."

"There is no tension," she snapped, crossing her arms. Big mistake. It drew my attention to the way her blouse hugged her breasts.

I tilted my head, giving her a slow, knowing look. "No tension? Then why'd you drag me in here?"

Before she could argue, a voice piped up from behind us. "Oh my God, they're flirting in the janitor's closet."

I turned to find my three-person delivery crew not-so-subtly peeking around the corner. Corben was blatantly recording on her phone, probably already drafting the submission email for *America's Funniest Videos.*

I pointed at her. "Delete that."

"Aww," Corben pouted but begrudgingly complied.

Quinn practically vibrated with excitement, clutching her hands over her chest. "You two are so cute."

Corben sighed dramatically. "They're like Zuko and Katara in *Avatar: The Last Airbender.*"

Quinn nodded eagerly. "Epic slow burn. They're destined to be together."

Samantha giggled. "Love fueled by shared pain and moments of vulnerability."

Mel shot me a look. "Should I be concerned that middle schoolers are plotting our love life?"

I grinned. "Probably. But I'd be more concerned that they clearly think you're the Katara in this situation."

Samantha gasped. "Oh my God, she so is."

Mel's face darkened slightly, her lips pressing into a thin line. "Go eat your lunch, girls. Ms. Nooney and I need to finish our conversation."

Quinn giggled. "Ooooh, Ms. Nooney. Someone's in trouble."

Samantha wiggled her eyebrows. "Is this where the slow burn turns into a forced proximity scene?"

Mel crossed her arms. "It's about to turn into a detention if you don't start moving."

Corben sighed, tucking her phone into her pocket. "Fine, fine. But just so you know, we're rooting for you both."

As they scurried off, Mel turned to me, exhaling sharply. "Look what you've done."

A smile tugged at my lips as I folded my arms. "You know, Mel, adults underestimate how well middle schoolers can read between the lines."

She scowled, sitting back and rubbing a hand over her face. "Bobby, we can't just let them think... whatever it is they're thinking."

I leaned forward, giving her a long look. "What exactly do you think they're thinking?"

Mel flushed, her lips twitching as she tried to maintain her composure. "That you and I are... some kind of romantic... couple."

I felt tension build in my chest but didn't back down. "Would that be so horrible?"

Mel shook her head, though her eyes lingered on me for a fraction longer than necessary. "We're educators."

"Right, right," I said, holding my hands up in mock surrender. "I'll try not to mix any more... unprofessional thoughts into my feelings for you."

Mel shot me a look. "Yes, try harder." Her usual steely gaze faltered ever so slightly, and for a brief moment, I caught a glimpse of uncertainty in the narrowing of her eyes. Her mouth quivered at the corners as if struggling to hide something.

She shifted her weight, one foot tapping subtly against the floor as her hand fidgeted with the keys on her lanyard. Every micro-expression whispered that her crisp command was layered with something more sensitive.

I could almost hear the tiny crack in her armor, a split-second pause before she crossed her arms and looked away.

"I have to go," she said, softer now, the steel in her voice giving way to something more fragile. Her eyes dropped for just a second, like she didn't want to see the look on my face. "Stop joking around, Bobby. I've kept my guard up for a reason. Real things get messy."

With one last, hesitant look over her shoulder, she fled.

As her footsteps faded, a storm churned inside me—confusion, longing, fear. Mel hadn't just walked away from a joke; she'd fled when things were about to get real. But deep down, I felt her silence wasn't a rejection. It was hesitation.

I could've chased her. Asked for answers. But I knew better. Pushing now wouldn't put only her emotions at risk. It would crack open everything I'd worked to keep buried.

The last time I let myself be fully seen, I lost my family. It left me shut out of the only place I'd ever called home.

Since then, I'd kept it light. Laugh it off, joke it away. But Mel made me wonder if I could cast off the armor. Pursuing her could wreck our friendship. But what if it didn't?

I wanted someone who saw all of me and stayed. I wanted a home again. I wanted Mel.

Chapter 7

Mel

The hum of the bus engine and the chatter of thirty-three rambunctious students filled the air, but my thoughts were stuck on something else entirely. Or rather, someone else.

Bobby.

Sitting across the aisle from me, she bounced between staring at me and her phone.

She'd been watching me all afternoon. Not in a casual we're just chaperoning way, but in a way that sent warmth curling low in my stomach. I felt it during the team-building challenge when our group worked to untangle a human knot. I noticed it when she stood a little too close, her arm brushing mine as we passed out pizza. And I caught it when I laughed with the kids—her lips parting like she was memorizing the sound.

It was unsettling. It was exhilarating. It was completely messing with my head.

I shifted in my seat, glancing sideways.

And there she was. Staring again.

Her short brown hair looked slightly tousled, like she'd just dragged her fingers through it. It framed her face in a disheveled way, drawing attention to the sharp lines of her cheekbones and the intensity of her deep-set brown eyes.

But it was her smile that undid me every time. Uninhibited and a little crooked, it was disarming. Just like the way she carried herself, confident without ever being loud. She didn't need to command a room to own it.

Bobby was nothing like Austin.

Austin had been all flash—charming smiles, sharp suits, and confidence that could sell a lie as easily as the truth. He had a way of making people feel special until they weren't. One minute, I'd been the center of his universe. The next I was a convenience he discarded when someone more exciting came along.

Bobby didn't use words to manipulate or distract. She was steady. Solid. A presence that didn't demand attention but held it anyway. And she watched me. Not like Austin had, as if I were something to possess, but like she saw me and wanted to know more. It was unsettling and exhilarating at the same time.

I shifted in my seat, glancing out the window as we sped down the highway toward the school. Slowly I slid my gaze over to where Bobby was sitting across the aisle.

And it hit me like a bolt of lightning. I'd let anger close me off, but I wasn't in that situation anymore. Not anymore. I was done second-guessing what I wanted and how people would react.

With Bobby, I didn't have to perform. I didn't have to be the one hold everything together. She'd slipped past my defenses, and if there was even the slightest chance that this could be real, I had to try. I had to take the risk.

"Hey," I said, patting the empty seat beside me. "Why don't you come sit over here? There's plenty of room."

She raised an eyebrow, a hint of a smile tugging at the corner of her mouth. "What's the catch?"

"No catch," I replied with a shrug, keeping my tone casual. "Just thought it might be nice to not have to shout across the aisle."

Her smile widened, and she pushed herself up, stepping across the aisle with easy grace despite the moving bus. She slid into the seat next to mine, our legs brushing as she settled in.

An awkward silence thickened between us, stretching uncomfortably as my mind scrambled for something to say. My pulse thudded in my ears, and the longer the quiet dragged on, the heavier it pressed against my chest. I hadn't thought this far ahead, and now, my mind was an empty chalkboard, wiped clean of any clever remark. I shifted my weight from one foot to the other, resisting the urge to fidget. Say something. Say anything.

Bobby finally broke the ice. "How do you think the SCA meeting went today?"

I was so relieved, I snorted. "Nothing says team spirit like a bunch of middle schoolers trying to untangle themselves."

"I'll never forget how you stepped over that tiny 6th grader and slid between Emma and Lincoln," she teased.

"Hey, it worked," I shot back, grinning. "We won."

She leaned back a little, eyes narrowing playfully. "Was it a competition?"

I chuckled, feeling the familiar spark of flirtation between us. "If it's not a competition, what's the point of playing?"

Bobby's gaze dropped to my lips for just a moment before she met my eyes again, a flicker of something unreadable passing over her face. "That's a very un-guidance counselor thing to say. Aren't you supposed to be all hold-hands-and-sing-*Kumbaya* or whatever?"

She tilted her head, the ghost of a smirk tugging at the corner of her mouth, but there was an edge to her voice. Was she teasing me... or testing me? Bobby could make the walls around anyone's heart crumble with nothing but a lopsided smile and a well-timed joke. And damn it, she got me. The air between us felt charged, a strange mix of challenge and curiosity.

I swallowed hard, trying to play it cool, forcing a chuckle even as my pulse quickened. "Only on Fridays. The rest of the week, I'm just trying to keep kids from committing social and emotional warfare in the hallways."

She let out a short laugh. "Sounds exhausting."

"You have no idea. Middle schoolers could teach the CIA a thing or two about psychological torture."

Bobby shook her head, amused. "And yet, you willingly signed up for this job?"

"Some people like skydiving. I thrive in the emotional minefield of adolescence." I shrugged. "We all have our kinks."

"Careful, Mel," she warned with a playful glint in her eye. "I'm gonna think you're flirting with me."

Flirting back was easy. Safer, even, if I kept it light and surface-level. No one ever walked away with a broken heart from flirting.

I leaned in slightly, our faces close enough that I could feel the heat between us. "Maybe I am," I whispered, my heart pounding just a little faster than usual.

Bobby's grin was slow, but it was all the answer I needed.

"So…" she started, her voice a little softer now. "Are we just gonna pretend the last time we talked didn't happen?"

My stomach clenched. I knew exactly what she meant. "For the record, I don't make a habit of yelling at people and then running away," I said, my tone light. "I figured you might have questions."

She swallowed, the clench and release of her throat fascinated me, but I looked up, trying to keep my expression neutral.

"Of course I have questions. But I'm also not sure I want the answers."

"I shouldn't have—" I stopped, rubbing a hand over my face before dropping it with a sigh. "I wasn't fair. I know that."

"I wasn't sending those notes to get under your skin, Mel." Bobby crossed my arms. "Well, I was, but only because I like you."

I pressed my lips together to hold back my laugh. She looked so worried. "I liked the poem you sent me."

She raised a brow. "Yeah?"

I sighed again, slower this time. "It made me..." I shook my head. "Forget it."

"Forget what?" she pressed.

I drew a breath, but it caught halfway. "I overreacted because I stopped seeing it as a game. I started waiting for your next move. I started caring." I looked away. "And that scared me more than I wanted to admit." "And that's a bad thing?" she asked, soft but curious, like she was already halfway through the door and just waiting to see if I'd open it the rest of the way.

A bad thing? No. But admitting it out loud felt like handing over the last piece of armor I had left. Intimacy could curdle into pain in a heartbeat, but I wasn't panicking. Not exactly. Just... calculating the fall-out. Running scenarios in my head.

My fingers twitched at my sides. "Not bad. Just... dangerous," I said quietly. "Somewhere between the notes and teasing, I forgot to keep my walls up. And I don't know how to pretend that they're still there."

My fingers dug into the skin of my palms as if bracing for impact. But I wouldn't turn away. My weight shifted toward her, my hip connecting with hers.

The rumble of the bus's engine cut through the quiet between us, and the kids' noise level grew even louder as we turned into the school. The rustling of backpacks and the scuff of sneakers against the floor signaled they were anxious to go home.

Bobby glanced toward the front as the driver pulled into the school's drop-off lane, but she didn't move. Her arms casually crossed over her chest, and her smile grew as she leaned back against the seat. Her legs stretched out, blocking me from getting up.

"You're not planning on keeping me here, are you?" I asked, arching an eyebrow as I half-turned toward her, trying not to smile.

Bobby raised an eyebrow, her smirk widening just a little. "What's the rush?"

"I've got a job, you know. Responsibilities. Small humans depending on me."

She leaned in, voice low and teasing. "Sounds important. But I think they can get off the bus on their own."

I rolled my eyes, but the heat creeping up my neck gave me away. "You're a bad influence."

"Not yet," she said with a grin. "But give me time."

I let out a small, forced laugh. "You won't let me leave?"

Bobby gave a small shrug. "I didn't say that. You just have to ask me nicely."

I huffed out a laugh, my heart still racing, but I was starting to enjoy the back-and-forth. "Fine," I said, then paused, leaning in a bit closer. "Bobby, would you please move?"

She tilted her head, looking down at me with a slight smirk. "You can do better than that."

I rolled my eyes. "Okay, how about this—if you don't move, I'm filing an official complaint with HR. For emotional sabotage."

Bobby chuckled, completely unfazed. "Pretty sure HR would take my side."

She stood, finally letting me pass, but not before her fingers brushed against mine just a second too long to be accidental.

The warmth of that fleeting touch stayed with me, curling around my ribs. I forced myself to keep moving, even as my hand twitched with the urge to reach back. Just to make sure I hadn't imagined it.

I stood near the driver at the front of the bus as students slowly made their way down the aisle, gathering their things and filing out.

"I had a great time tonight. Be sure to say thank you to Ms. Nooney and our bus driver, Pam."

"Miss B! You owe me a rematch in Uno at the next meeting," a seventh-grader called out.

I turned, flashing what I hoped was an easy grin. "Only if you promise not to cry when I destroy you, Cooper."

"Pfft. You got lucky."

Amy rolled her eyes. "My parents are over there. Can I go now?"

"We're keeping you here all night," Bobby teased, stepping into the aisle to block her way, and the girl groaned in dramatic agony.

When the bus doors whooshed open, the kids filed out. I followed them, making sure parents and students were reunited and everyone had a ride home.

"So," she said, stuffing her hands into her pockets. "Would you like to go drink?" She blinked. "I mean—for a drink. Unless you want to go drinking. In which case, I'm also in."

Her cheeks turned pink. A sign that Bobby wasn't as confident as she seemed, and I watched her fumble for the right words as a strange warmth curled in my chest.

"Smooth," I said, raising an eyebrow. "Is that your official invitation technique?"

No matter how much I tried to keep things cool and distant, Bobby broke through my barriers. It was terrifying, but I couldn't hide away. Not this time.

I ran a hand through my hair and met her eyes, steady now, ignoring the flutter in my chest. I knew I was toeing the line—but I wasn't running anymore.

Not from her. Not from myself.

"You buying?" I asked, letting the corners of my mouth lift just enough.

It wasn't just a question. It was a beginning.

Chapter 8

Bobby

I took a slow sip of my drink, the whiskey warm as it slid down, but not nearly as warm as the way Mel was looking at me. The candle between us flickered, throwing soft shadows across her face, and for a second, I forgot how to breathe.

She was beautiful. Her calm, steady gaze made me feel seen in a way I wasn't used to. The tension from earlier had faded, but something quieter had taken its place. Closer. Her smile wasn't big, but it reached her eyes, and that alone unraveled something in me.

"So," I started, leaning in just a little, "what's the real reason you became a guidance counselor?"

Mel gave a small, wry smile. "Honestly? I didn't think I had many options." She let out a soft laugh, more self-aware than amused. "I stopped teaching while I was married, so going back to the classroom didn't feel right. I decided to go back to school to get my guidance degree. Turns out, I'm good at it."

Her casual mention of her marriage caught me off guard, and a tightness gripped my chest. "What was your marriage like?"

Mel stiffened just a fraction, her fingers curling around her glass as she stared into it for a moment before meeting my gaze. "Austin and I dated in high school. We grew apart during college, but then I bumped into him again while I was teaching high school in Roanoke. We dated for a while, and when he asked me to marry him, I thought it would be forever."

Heat crawled up my neck, my pulse quickening as a knot of jealousy twisted tight in my gut. It didn't seem fair—this image of her with someone else, her heart tied up with another person.

Her expression was distant as she said, "It was good for a while. I stopped teaching, and we tried to have a baby. But it was hard for me to get pregnant, and I had a few miscarriages. I fell into a pretty deep depression. It wasn't a great time for me." She paused, her eyes losing focus for a moment.

"I'm really sorry you went through that," I said softly, meeting her eyes. I reached across the table, my fingers brushing hers in a quiet offer of comfort. "You didn't deserve that kind of pain. Thank you for trusting me with it."

Her gaze flickered down to where our hands touched, but she didn't pull away.

"Austin... he didn't know how to handle it. So, he turned to other women."

Anger sliced through me, and I had to fight the urge to say something sharp might hurt more than help. Instead, I just watched her, my heart aching for her, wishing I could take away the pain she was still carrying.

She took a slow breath, her eyes drifting past me before refocusing. "And then he died, and I was so angry. I moved in with my mom and threw myself into work. But Roanoke's basically a small town, and everyone knew what happened. I needed to get out. Start over." She shrugged, a small, tired smile tugging at her mouth. "I'm okay now. I adopted a dog and let go of that part of my life."

I leaned in with a smile. "Wait. You're just going to drop a dog reveal like that? What kind of dog?"

She laughed, the tension easing from her shoulders. "Moose is a golden retriever mix."

"Moose?" I repeated, eyebrows raised. "That's a bold name for a dog."

"He earned it," she said, her smile growing. "He's huge, clumsy, and thinks he's a lapdog. Follows me everywhere, cries when I close the bathroom door, and sheds like it's his job. But he's sweet."

"So, let me get this straight," I said, teasing. "You're telling me the emotionally distant guidance counselor goes home to a 90-pound cuddle monster?"

Mel gave a faux glare. "Shut up. He's therapeutic."

"I bet he is," I said, grinning. "I'm just saying, if Moose likes me, I'm taking that as a sign."

As I said it, my mind caught on the way she smiled when she talked about Moose, how it softened the sharp edges of her usual guarded self. She'd let me in, just a little, and it felt important. Maybe she was beginning to trust me.

"So, what about you?" she asked, her voice low but steady, pulling me in like a magnet. "Tell me a little about your past."

I blinked. Mel looked at me a steady, unflinching gaze, and for a second, I forgot how to breathe. She was waiting for me to answer.

I took a deep breath, the weight of old memories pressing in on me, like an invitation to finally let them out.

"Well," I started, my voice quieter than usual, "when I was in Afghanistan, there was this one time—"

I paused, the words coming slower than I expected. It wasn't something I talked about often, but with Mel, it felt right. "My friend Oz and I were stationed near the Afghan palace at Camp Eggers when we got word there might be an attack that night."

I glanced down, my voice quieter. "Oz... he isn't just a friend. He's my people. You know? The kind of person who shows up when your own family can't or won't. He reminded me that you can still build a life worth living, even if it doesn't look like the one you came from."

I exhaled slowly, the memory heavy on my chest. "Anyway, the constant threat of violence wears on you. It's not until things go to hell that you realize how much you've taken for granted—simple things, like breathing without fear. We were all on edge, waiting. Then, out of nowhere, Oz pulls out a deck of cards and starts dealing like it's the most normal thing in the world. It was ridiculous—but exactly what we needed. For an hour, we played cards, laughed, and talked about everything except war. It was just us, holding on to our humanity in the middle of hell."

Mel's eyes didn't leave mine. She nodded slowly, her voice quiet but sure. "Funny how something so simple can keep you grounded, even in the worst of times."

She paused, then added, "I'm glad Oz was there for you. Family isn't always the people we're born to. It's the ones who stay, especially when things fall apart."

Her words hung between us as I swallowed down emotion. Mel had seen a part of me I'd kept buried since my family turned their backs on me.

I cleared my throat, forcing a smile that didn't quite reach my eyes. "Yeah, well... thanks."

She didn't say anything right away, just held my gaze. Finally, she gave a small nod, like she was giving me permission to let it go.

Just as the silence between us felt like it was about to settle into something comfortable, the door to the bar creaked open, and a familiar woman's voice sliced through the quiet. "Well, well, well, look who's here."

My head snapped up, and I took in the wide grins of Val, Audrey, and Keith hovering just inside the restaurant doorway.

Great. Our coworkers had arrived just in time to turn this moment with Mel into a full-blown sitcom.

Across from me, Mel stiffened, her posture going ramrod straight. Her hand darted to her glass, and she took a quick sip.

Walking toward us, Val wiggled her eyebrows. Audrey bit her lip, clearly trying not to laugh, and Keith offered a clueless little wave.

I fought the urge to groan. So much for quiet vulnerability and emotionally grounded conversations.

Mel was already retreating behind her polite smile, and I could feel her slipping just out of reach.

Audrey's eyes danced. "Look at you guys out on the town," she called out, practically bouncing over to our table.

Keith wasn't far behind. "Can we join the party?" He paused, squinting at us both like he was trying to figure out if we were about to drop a bombshell. "Wait, wait. Are you two having a moment here?"

Mel gave me a glance like she wasn't sure whether to dive under the table or laugh it off. I couldn't help but notice the way her posture straightened, clearly trying to regain some composure. Her lips twitched like she was about to say something sarcastic, but instead, she just let out a soft laugh.

"Sure, join us." I gestured to the empty chairs. "We're just unwinding after surviving a field trip with the SCA—no casualties, but emotionally? We've aged five years."

Val plopped herself down next to Mel. "Careful, Mel—if you smile any harder when Bobby's around, people are gonna start writing fanfiction," she teased, nudging Mel.

Mel's eyes crinkled just slightly with amusement, and Val leaned in with that easy, conspiratorial grin like we were in on the same joke.

Sipping my drink, I let their conversation wash over me. For once, I didn't feel like I had to brace myself for impact. I let myself believe I belonged.

Audrey nudged Val. "So, who had Bobby Gives Mel Goo-Goo Eyes on their bingo card?"

Val raised a hand. "I mean, I didn't not expect it."

Mel gave them her best scolding look. "You two done?"

I laughed. "Please, don't stop on my account. I'm enjoying this roast in real time."

"Good," Val said. "Because we weren't gonna stop."

Their teasing wrapped around me like a favorite sweatshirt—familiar, a little ridiculous, and impossible not to smile through. This was what I'd been craving since I first rolled into Marchfield. Connection. Friends who saw me and didn't flinch. Who wouldn't bail at the drop of a hat.

And here they were, flinging sarcasm like it was a love language. Like I'd always been part of the rhythm.

Mel caught my eye, her smirk softening into something more private.

They'd pulled me into their orbit, wrapped me into their friendship like it was second nature, and it meant more than I could say. So, I didn't try. I just sat back, let myself be teased, and soaked it in like sunlight I hadn't known I was starving for.

Keith dropped his menu with theatrical flair, sighing so loudly half the restaurant turned. "I tried to text you so you could meet us, but nooo—you were already out gallivanting without your emotional support crew."

Val leaned in, clutching her chest like she'd been personally wronged. "We're not mad you ditched us. We just cried, lit a candle, and started a group chat called *Bobby's Betrayal.*"

Audrey raised her glass. "First meeting's Thursday. We'll be processing our collective trauma over nachos."

I rolled my eyes, but the laugh slipped out before I could stop it. "Wow. One date and I'm a villain?"

"A charismatic one," Keith said, tossing a peanut at me. "But a villain nonetheless."

Mel was biting her lip, clearly trying not to laugh and failing. The sight of it knocked something loose in my chest.

These people saw me. Not the version I'd spent years perfecting. Me. And they didn't flinch. Didn't hesitate to pull me in and make me theirs.

Yeah. I could definitely get used to this.

Chapter 9

Mel

Barrel buzzed with conversations and laughter around us as Bobby and I squeezed together, making room for Audrey, Val, and Keith. Audrey, ever the instigator, made a move to slide between us, but Bobby scooted closer to me, pressing our sides together. "Nice try," she said with a smirk. "But my girlfriend sits next to me."

Heat flooded my face, my heart stuttering at the casual way she said it. As if it was obvious, a fact that she and I were together.

The word girlfriend sent a thrill through me, but it was tangled up with something fragile and uncertain. Did everyone else hear it the same way I did? Would they see me differently now? Would they whisper about us? That quiet fear curled around the edges of my joy.

With Austin, things had been simpler, or at least they looked that way from the outside. He'd been the easy choice, the expected one. Being bi in rural Virginia hadn't felt safe, so I clung to the part of me that passed, that fit neatly into everyone's expectations.

But being with Bobby was more real. More me.

And that was terrifying. Because for the first time, everything was out in the open. And I didn't know who that made me, or if the world was ready to see this new me.

"Did you just call Mel your girlfriend?" Audrey planted her elbows on the table, eyes sparkling with mischief. "Are we witnessing history tonight?"

Bobby shrugged and squeezed my hand under the table. "It's new."

"New," Keith echoed, smirking. "Or, like, an experiment?"

An experiment? Like I was just trying this out. Like Bobby was some phase I'd wake up from. The old panic stirred, tight and hot in my chest.

My fingers tightened around my glass, the condensation slick beneath my palm. The warmth of Bobby's hand suddenly felt far away, like I was drifting from something safe.

But before I could say anything, Bobby's voice cut through Keith's laughter, low but firm. "Shut up, Keith."

"What?" He looked between us, confused. "I didn't mean—"

Audrey's smile vanished as she turned to Keith. "Seriously? That's not funny."

Keith held up his hands. "Okay, okay—bad joke."

"Yeah," Val added, giving him a sharp look. "Really bad."

Why did one stupid comment make me feel like I was standing on unsteady ground? The laughter that had just moments ago felt warm and welcoming sounded distant. I was back in that small town again, where people smiled to my face and whispered behind my back.

I reached for my drink, mostly to keep my hands busy. My pulse thrummed in my ears, and the tightness in my chest made it hard to breathe. I hated how easily one line unraveled me.

"I'm gonna head out," I said, too fast, already scooting my chair back. I couldn't sit here another minute pretending I wasn't spiraling.

Bobby shifted beside me. "Mel—hey. Don't go."

Her voice was calm, grounding, but it only made the knot in my throat worse. I couldn't look at her. Not yet.

"Yeah," Val chimed in. "Don't let this idiot ruin your night."

"She's right, I am an idiot. I'm sorry—" Keith stood, reaching out to me.

Audrey gave me a gentler look. "We're not judging you, Mel. We're here. All in. Okay?"

Their words reached me, but they hit against something brittle. I wanted to believe them. God, I did. But the old armor crept back in, fast and familiar.

I stood up anyway. "I'm just tired. Nothing a good night's sleep won't fix."

Bobby's eyes met mine, searching for emotions hidden in their depths. Finally, she said, "You'll text me when you get home?"

"Sure," I said, standing up. "I'll be fine. Don't worry."

I wasn't sure if I was lying to her or to myself, but it didn't matter. I just needed to get out of there before I let my doubts swallow me whole.

After I got home, I barely had time to drop my keys on the entryway table before Moose trotted over from the living room, his nails clicking on the hardwood as he nudged my thigh with his nose. I sank to the floor beside him, pressing my face into his fur. He let out a soft huff and leaned into me.

My phone buzzed with an incoming call from Bobby. Her name lit up the screen, and for a second, I just stood there, torn. I wasn't ready. Not yet. My thoughts were still tangled, my chest tight with the weight of old fears and new feelings.

"Let's take a walk, huh?" I said, the magic words prompting a wolfish grin from Moose and an enthusiastic thump of his tail. I grabbed his leash, and we stepped out into the warm night, the hush of the neighborhood wrapping around us.

We wandered for a while, the quiet broken only by the soft scuff of my boots on pavement and the jingle of Moose's collar. By the time we returned, the tight knot in my chest had loosened a little, and my thoughts felt clearer—less like a storm and more like scattered clouds finally parting.

I needed someone who could remind me of who I was before the noise in my head got too loud. I pulled out my phone again, bypassed Bobby's messages, and tapped my mom's contact instead.

"Hey, Mom," I said as soon as she picked up, my voice small and wavering.

"Melody, sweetheart, are you alright?" The sound of her voice was comforting, like a warm blanket, and I felt a sudden rush of tenderness. For a brief moment, I was five again, sitting on the floor with skinned knees, knowing that no matter what, my mom would make it all better.

I sank onto the edge of my bed, letting the silence stretch for a moment before I began.

"Tonight was... a lot," I admitted into the quiet, my voice barely above a whisper.

There was a pause on the line, just long enough to let me know she was listening. Really listening.

"I was at the bar with Bobby and some friends," I continued, rubbing the back of my neck. "And for the most part it was great. Like, really great." I let out a short laugh that didn't quite land. "And then Keith—he made this offhand comment about me and Bobby. He asked if we were just... experimenting."

I swallowed hard. "I know he didn't mean it to sound cruel, but it hit me harder than I expected. Like he was saying what I feel for Bobby isn't real. Or worse, that it isn't normal." I paused, the words catching in my throat. "Like being with a woman is some kind of phase I'm trying on instead of something that's just me."

I exhaled, my voice smaller now. "It made me feel like I had to justify who I am. Like I don't get to just exist and be loved the way everyone else does."

I paused again, closing my eyes. "And the worst part? For a second, I believed him."

"Honey," Mom said as I took a shaky breath, brushing away tears that burned in the corners of my eyes. "You're true friends will support you and the rest can... well, they can go fuck themselves."

I let out a watery giggle. "I've spent my life hiding behind society's expectations. I leaned into my cisgender to avoid the scrutiny of being gay."

There was a gentle pause on the other end of the line, filled with unspoken understanding. "Melody, love isn't about fitting into neat little boxes or forcing yourself to be someone you're not. If your heart's chosen Bobby, then grab onto that love with both hands and don't let go."

Her soothing words eased the tight knot in my chest. I hesitated, my voice barely more than a whisper. "Mom... it all feels too overwhelming. What if I'm too scared?"

"Never surrender your inner strength to anyone," Mom reassured me, "You're resilient. Don't ever allow anyone to dim that light within you."

I closed my eyes, letting her steady voice seep into me. None of this was about my being bi—it was simply about the undeniable love I felt for Bobby. "Thanks, Mom," I managed, a small smile fighting through the lingering uncertainty. "I really needed to hear that."

"Believe it, baby. In your heart of hearts, believe it," she replied warmly before we ended the call. For a long moment, I sat in the quiet of my room, absorbing her words. Slowly, I pulled on my favorite worn black and white spotted pajamas with cows on them and *I'm Sexy and I Moo It* printed on the front.

I padded through the narrow hallway of my small rental. The soft glow of a single lamp illuminated framed photos and gentle floral wallpaper. The familiar creaks of the wooden floor and the low hum of the refrigerator were a quiet comfort as I made myself a cup of tea.

I had just settled on the couch when Moose scrambled toward the door, nails clicking on the hardwood, his tail a blur. Three seconds later, the doorbell rang.

My heart jumped because I already knew who it would be. And when I opened the door, there she was.

Bobby stood on the threshold, her eyes full of quiet concern, a small bouquet of wildflowers in one hand. Before I could say anything, Moose barreled past me and shoved his snout into Bobby's free hand.

She laughed, crouching to greet him. "Hey, buddy. Good to meet you."

Moose gave an approving huff and trotted back inside like he'd personally vetted Bobby and she had passed.

Her steady, unwavering gaze found mine, and her presence pulled me in like the tide. And all the noise in my head quieted. And love swept through me.

Our eyes met in the charged silence.

"I'm sorry about Keith." Bobby's voice trembled between anger and concern. "I nearly lost it—I even threatened to punch him."

Her words, raw and honest, deepened the intensity between us. I reached out, brushing my palm along her jaw. "Come in," I whispered, inviting her into the sanctuary of my home.

Closing the door behind her, I moved closer. The soft glow of the lamp bathed her in a warm light, and with every inch I gained, I felt the weight of my doubts dissolve into something tender and electric. Vulnerability and desire intertwined, urging me to let go and embrace the intimacy building between us.

Her hand, warm and sure, found the small of my back, drawing me in. The soft glow of my living room caught the curve of her smile, igniting a spark that set my skin alight.

For a heartbeat, we stood there, the space between us vibrating with unspoken desire. Bobby reached out, gently tucking a stray lock of hair behind my ear, her fingers caressing the sensitive spot there. "I don't care what anyone else thinks," she murmured, her voice low and rough. "Do you?"

My breath caught, but it wasn't fear that held me still. It was my desire and the undeniable gravity between us. I swallowed hard, my voice barely above a whisper. "No."

A slow, knowing smile curved her lips as she slid her hand up my spine. "Ask me to stay."

My pulse hammered in my throat. I wanted this. Wanted her.

"Stay."

Chapter 10

Mel

Her fingers threaded through my hair as she pressed me gently back against the wall. The solid weight of her, the steady, intoxicating warmth of her body against mine, made my knees weak.

Then she pulled back just enough to glance down, her eyes twinkling.

"Are those... cows?" she asked, grinning as she tugged lightly at the hem of my pajama top. "You seduce me in a pair of cow pajamas and expect me to survive?"

I huffed a laugh, cheeks burning. "They were clean."

Bobby leaned in again, her mouth brushing my ear. "Dangerous move, Mel. I have a thing for questionable sleepwear."

I choked on my laugh when her hands skimmed down my sides, gripping my waist. My fingers found the collar of her jacket, tugging the zipper down and sliding the fabric off her shoulders.

"Mel," she murmured against my lips, my name wrapped in something that made my pulse stutter.

I didn't want to think. Didn't want to question or hesitate. I just wanted her.

Tangling my fingers in her shirt, I marveled at the feel of her muscles as I pulled her flush against me. Every point of contact sent sparks skittering through my veins, and every slow, teasing brush of her lips against mine drove me closer to the edge.

"I've never.. I don't..." She needed to know this wasn't hesitation. It wasn't doubt. It was me stepping into something I'd spent years denying myself. "I've never been with..."

Bobby stilled, her breath warm against my lips. She pulled back just enough to look at me, her dark eyes searching mine with tenderness.

"You don't have to say anything," she murmured, her fingers brushing the curve of my cheek. "We go at your pace, Mel."

Bobby made me feel in a way I couldn't ignore. I swallowed hard, my fingers still curled in the fabric of her shirt. "I want to."

She exhaled, slow and measured, like she was holding herself back. "Then tell me what you like."

The heat in her voice sent a shiver down my spine. My body knew the answer before my lips could form the words. Sliding my hands over her shoulders, up into her short hair, I pulled her into a kiss that left no room for doubt.

Her hands skimmed down my sides, stopping at my waist, thumbs stroking soft circles against my skin. She was patient, giving me space, but I could feel the tension coiled in her body, the restraint in the way she held me.

I pressed closer, tilting my head, letting myself drown in the taste of her. My pulse thrummed as she groaned against my lips, her hands flexing against my hips.

"Mel," she whispered, her voice wrecked.

There were no words for everything I felt in that moment—the nerves, the hunger, the fear, the need.

Bobby groaned low in her throat, the sound sending a delicious shiver through me. Her mouth trailed along my jaw, down the curve of my neck, her teeth grazing the sensitive skin just enough to make me gasp. I tilted my head back, giving her more, needing more, and Bobby chuckled softly. The knowing, wicked sound sent heat pooling low in my belly.

Her hands slid under the hem of my pajama shirt, fingertips tracing lazy circles against my skin, teasing but not rushing. She was taking her time, savoring every touch, every reaction, and it was making me dizzy.

I caught her wrist, my breath coming fast, my heart pounding so hard it felt like it might break free of my ribs. "Bobby..."

She stilled, her lips hovering just above mine, her dark eyes searching my face. "Tell me what you want."

The words sent a fresh wave of heat through me, desire curling tight and insistent. I swallowed, my fingers tightening on her wrist as I met her gaze. Leading her back to my bedroom, I could feel her eyes on me.

Turning to face her with my back to the bed, I stripped my pajama top off. "I want you."

Bobby's breath hitched. Then she kissed me again while she stroked up my sides to cup my breasts. When she rolled my nipples between her fingers, my knees went weak and a moan slipped from my mouth.

She shoved my pajama pants down, pushing me back onto the bed. A grin split her lips as she lowered herself down next to me.

"I swear I shaved this morning," I said with a nervous laugh, "No unexpected surprises down there."

Bobby raised an eyebrow, a teasing smile playing on her lips. "Well, now I'm intrigued. Should I inspect for myself?"

Her fingers traced the bare skin of my hip, slow and deliberate, leaving a trail of fire in their wake. The weight of her gaze pinned me in place, her grin shifting into something darker, something knowing.

"You sure?" Bobby murmured, her breath ghosting over my cheek.

I swallowed hard, my pulse hammering. "Yeah." My voice wavered from force of wanting her.

She dipped her head, pressing open-mouthed kisses along my jaw, down my throat to my breasts. Every touch unraveled me, every shift of her body against mine sent a fresh wave of heat rolling through me.

Her lips closed over my nipple, sucking hard as I arched toward her, my heels digging into the mattress. I clutched at her shoulders as she dipped further down, settling between my legs.

Pressure built deep inside me, gathering at the base of my spine and then lower as her tongue and teeth rasped over my clit. Bobby's fingers found me, stroking in just the right rhythm and speed. She listened to my body, adjusting with each gasp, moan, and shiver to give me more pleasure.

I reached for her blindly, grappling with Bobby's shirt and bra until the heat of her skin melted against mine.

"Bobby—" I gasped, one breath away from climax. One moment before she pushed me up and over into oblivion.

My eyes squeezed shut as I shuddered. The intensity of emotion and feeling collided, my body quaking.

"Look at me, Mel," Bobby commanded as she moved up beside me, and I obeyed.

My eyes took in her strong, lithe body. Her firm breasts tipped with brown nipples. The creamy skin stretched down to her jeans, the dark fabric a stark contrast to her skin.

A long, jagged scar on her left shoulder caught my attention, a silent reminder that Bobby hadn't always walked the safest path in life. I leaned in and kissed the old injury, my lips tracing the edge of it as if somehow I could erase the past. She sighed softly, her body responding to my touch.

"Does it still hurt?" I asked quietly, my fingers brushing over the scar.

Bobby shrugged, as if she was used to the past lingering like that. "Not really."

I started to ask how she was wounded, but she cut me off with a sly grin. "Are we doing story time, or are you going to kiss me?"

I grinned back, shaking my head. "I think you've earned a few more kisses."

My lips brushed hers again, soft and teasing at first, but quickly melted into a deeper heat between with every press and tug. I could feel her smile against my mouth as my hand slid to the back of her neck.

Flipping open the button to her jeans, I slid the zipper down, the urgency of my touch a silent demand. Shimmying the fabric down over her hips, her jeans dropped to the floor, and my eyes widened at her bare pussy.

"You wax?" I asked breathlessly, desperate to explore the bare skin.

"I take a monthly trip to Brazil." Bobby's smirk made me snort. "Do you like it?"

"I do," I said, allowing my hand to slid down between her legs. The silky softness welcomed me, her clit begging to be stroked.

Circling my thumb around her center, I delighted in watching Bobby succumb to pleasure. She was so usually so strong and in control that it shocked and excited me to see the power I held over her.

I sampled every part of her, the sweet heat of her mouth to the wet neediness of her clit. I teased and explored, letting my hands and lips learn her in a way I had never been able to with Austin. With him, there had always been a script, an expectation. But with Bobby, it was all discovery—raw, intoxicating, and entirely ours.

She gasped, then laughed breathlessly. "You're really trying to ruin me, aren't you?"

I glanced up, grinning. "Not ruin. Just... recalibrate your standards."

Bobby's fingers slid into my hair, tugging gently. "Oh, they're shot to hell already. Congratulations."

I kissed the inside of her thigh. "Good. Means I'm doing something right."

And somewhere between her laughter and the way she looked at me like I was not a secret, not a phase, but hers, I realized I'd found it. That fresh start I I'd been searching for was right here.

The weight of old wounds loosened. The fear that love had to come with conditions faded. The past didn't vanish—but it stopped defining me.

And I let myself believe that this could be home.

Bobby's orgasm rocked us both. Her body stretched taut, vibrating with each wave of pleasure. Her voice cracked on my name, her arms locking around me tight.

The strength of it brought my own need the edge again. She reversed our roles, lifting me higher.

The words slipped out, a gasp of truth that I hadn't even realized I was holding back. "I love you," I whispered, clutching her shoulders as if saying it would somehow anchor me in the sea of pleasure.

Bobby stilled for a heartbeat, her dark eyes locking with mine, intense and wide. "Say it again," she demanded, her voice low, almost reverent.

I smiled, the weight of the words settling into me like a familiar warmth. "I love you," I said again, this time with a teasing glint in my eye. "More than I've ever loved anyone."

In an instant, her mouth was on me, circling my clit with her tongue. Pleasure edged with pain as she drove me further and further toward climax.

And then I was flying across a glittering sea of pleasure. And Bobby was beside me. She brushed a strand of hair from my face, her thumb grazing my cheek. Her voice was steady and serious. "I love you, too, Mel."

Chapter 11

Bobby

The gym smelled like a mix of vinegar, burnt sugar, and something vaguely metallic—the result of at least one ill-advised experiment. The Marchfield Spring Science Fair was in full swing, and I was running on nothing but caffeine and sheer willpower.

At table five, two sixth graders eagerly explained their hypothesis on whether a betta fish could recognize human faces. Their findings? Inconclusive. The fish spent more time posturing for his own reflection than studying the lineup of printed selfies that were taped to the tank.

Further down, an eighth grader demonstrated what he promised was "a totally safe, controlled explosion." I hovered near the fire extinguisher just in case.

And then there was table twelve. A seventh grader had built what she called a "mood-reading machine" that supposedly determined emotions based on body temperature and pulse. Except every time I placed my hand on the sensor, the screen blinked UNSURE in big red letters.

Accurate.

The doors to the gym banged open, letting in a shaft of warm sunlight that caught in the dust like gold.

And Mel rushed in, breathless, her bag slipping off her shoulder. Her hair was wind-tousled, cheeks flushed from the spring air, and she wore a soft green cardigan over a soft dress that fluttered past her knees.

She scanned the room, and when her eyes found mine, she smiled. Everything in the room faded as I absorbed it—warm, a little crooked, and so full of so much love, it knocked the breath from my lungs.

"You're late," I said, arching a brow.

"Sorry, sorry! I got stuck behind a tractor hauling an entire parade float covered in plastic flamingos. Then, when I finally got around it, I had to stop again because Sandy Richardson's emotional support goat was standing in the middle of Main Street, refusing to move. Animal Control finally showed up, but *Sir Bleats A Lot* jumped onto their truck and started eating their paperwork." She grinned. "Tardy pass, no questions asked?"

I sighed, handing her a clipboard. "Fine. But you're judging table seven. It's a study on how much saliva different candies produce."

Mel groaned but took the clipboard anyway. "You're cruel."

I smirked. "Science can be disgusting."

Noise of the fair swirled around us, and I couldn't help but feel a flicker of pride. This might have been my first year teaching, but somehow, I'd almost survived. Barely. And if I could make it through the next thirty minutes, I could make it through the remaining three weeks until summer.

After what felt like hours of circuits, slime, and far too many exploding volcanoes, it was finally time to announce the winners.

I climbed onto a chair and clapped my hands. "All right, science geniuses, let's wrap this up!" The students gathered around, buzzing with excitement as I read off the winners.

"For Most Creative Hypothesis... our goldfish psychology team!" The two sixth graders cheered.

"For Best Use of the Scientific Method... the candy spit experiment!" Mel made a face as the proud eighth grader fist-bumped his friends.

"For Best Unintended Consequences... the seventh graders who tried to grow mold on different types of bread and accidentally created a biohazard." I waved toward the project, which was quarantined inside a Ziploc bag after bringing on two allergy asthma attacks.

"For Most Surprisingly Successful Experiment... the group who proved you can cook an egg on a car hood in May, but only if you use a magnifying glass and wait two hours." The trio of kids responsible cheered, one of them still wearing oven mitts from their demonstration.

"And finally, for Most Likely to Result in an Accidental Detention... our totally-safe-explosion guy!" The crowd whooped as he raised his arms in victory. I just hoped he didn't take that as encouragement to escalate his experiments next year.

Once the last ribbon was handed out and parents had rounded up their kids, the real work began. Cleanup.

Mel swept up a pile of fluffy white powder while I started folding up chairs. She eyed it warily. "I really hope no one walks in right now. This looks like we're running a very poorly funded drug operation."

I snorted. "Yeah, but instead of cocaine, it's just cornstarch and crushed dreams."

The other science teachers, Dee O'Malley and John Ling, carted away trifold boards, unplugged hot plates, and peeled dried glue off the tables. One by one, people trickled out, until Mel and I were alone under the buzzing gym lights.

Stacking the last of the chairs, I turned to her, smirking. "Ms. Brannaghan, we never finished that lesson on kinetic energy."

Mel stilled, her hands still gripping the edge of the table. A slow, blush crept up her neck. "Oh?"

I took a deliberate step forward, closing the space between us, closing in on her until her back touched the folded up bleachers. My palms flattened against the cool metal on either side of her.

"Mmhm." I leaned in, my lips just a breath away from hers. "Want to do some... experiments?"

Mel let out a shaky laugh, her hands sliding up my arms. "That depends."

"On?"

Her voice dropped to a whisper. "Are we testing velocity... or combustion?"

I grinned, then kissed her—deep, slow, and thorough, stealing whatever breath she had left. Her body went soft against mine, every inch of her molding to me, as if she couldn't get close enough. Her fingers tangled in the fabric of my shirt, tugging me tighter, pulling me deeper into the kiss, her lips moving against mine in perfect sync. The world around us faded, the only sound the sharp, quick rush of our breaths and the steady thump of my heart racing to keep up.

The heat between us was undeniable and electric, humming through me with her every touch, every movement. Her skin was like fire, and I was drawn to her like a moth.

My hands trailed down her sides, pulling her closer, until I felt the press of her body against me. Every curve, every inch of her, seared through my clothes to my skin.

She broke away, gasping for air, her chest rising and falling rapidly. Her eyes were darker now, filled with raw, hungry emotion. Her voice was a low, breathless whisper. "You're trouble, you know that?"

I chuckled, my fingers brushing a lock of hair from her face as I leaned in close again, my lips just a breath away from hers. "You liked trouble."

She rolled her eyes, but I saw the smile tug at her lips. "Depends on the type."

Instead of kissing her again right away, I hesitated for a breath, and reached for the chain around my neck. The old brass key, warm from resting against my skin, slid into my fingers. I'd worn it for weeks, trying to find the right moment to give it to Mel.

It wasn't just a key. It was a piece of armor I hadn't realized I was ready to take off.

"On my first day," I murmured, slipping the old brass key from around my neck, "I was locked out of more than just a classroom. My parents wouldn't accept me. My friends were miles away. I felt completely alone. But you—" I met her eyes, my voice catching just slightly, "—Mel, you helped me build a new family here in Marchfield."

She stared at me. Her breath caught, her lips parting slightly, so I pressed the key gently into her hand. "This is the spare to my place. But it's also me saying... Thank you, Mel for helping me unlock the door to my heart. I love you."

Her fingers curled around the key, and a teasing smile tugged at the corner of her mouth. "Are you proposing I move in, or is this so I can steal the last chocolate Pop-Tart without knocking?"

I laughed, but I didn't look away. "Both. You always have a place with me."

Mel looked down at the key, then back up at me. She stepped in close, voice barely above a whisper. "I love you too, Bobby."

Leaning in I brushed my lips across hers—barely a touch, just enough to drive her wild. A shiver ran down her spine, and then she pulled me in by the collar of my shirt, her lips meeting mine with a force that made my head spin.

I tangled my hands in her hair, pulling her closer as the kiss deepened, the tension between us building until it was almost unbearable. My heart was pounding in my chest, and I knew if we didn't stop soon, we wouldn't stop at all.

"Bobby," she breathed, breaking the kiss, her voice shaky but filled with desire. She looked up at me, her eyes wild, lips swollen from our kiss. "We're... Are we really doing this?"

I could feel the heat of her body, her chest rising against mine as she searched my face for any sign of hesitation. But there was none. There was nothing but her, nothing but the pull between us that felt like it was meant to be.

"We've already done more than enough to get ourselves into trouble," I said, my voice rough, my hand sliding down the curve of her waist.

She was ravishing. Her face was flushed, cheeks dusted with color that deepened the curve of her cheekbones. Stray golden brown curls clung to her temples, wild and damp from the heat between us. Her lips were parted, kiss-bruised and glistening, and her eyes—God, her eyes—were locked on mine, dark purple and molten with hunger. She looked like a storm just starting to break—wild, beautiful, and entirely unstoppable.

"You always do this to me," she whispered.

I raised an eyebrow, still catching my breath. "What, kiss you silly?"

She grinned, her fingers trailing along my jaw. "No. Make me forget how I ever lived without you."

My breath hitched, and I leaned into her touch. "Good," I murmured. "Because I don't plan on letting you remember."

Her eyes sparkled, lips parting with a comeback I never got to hear because right then, the gym door clanged open.

We scrambled apart, stifling laughter and adjusting our clothes like two teenagers caught behind the bleachers instead of two allegedly responsible adults who hadn't been making out behind the science fair volcano.

The sound of heavy footsteps echoed across the gym floor, and a low voice called out, "Hey, anyone there?"

Mr. Holman, the custodian, had a slow, shuffling gait and a constant, knowing smile. He wore his faded navy jumpsuit with the sleeves rolled up, the name tag hanging loosely from the pocket. His mop, already dripping with water, swayed behind him as he pushed the door open with his foot, the squeak of the hinges cutting through the stillness of the room.

He gave us a half-smile, raising an eyebrow as he leaned against the doorframe, his gaze flicking between us. "You know, I was starting to think you two had gone without saying goodbye, but then I saw your cars still parked outside." His grin was wide. He knew exactly what he'd interrupted.

"Just finishing up," I blurted, trying to sound casual while my pulse threatened to escape my chest. I ran a hand through my hair, hoping I didn't look like I was about to combust.

Mr. Holman winked. "Sure, sure. I'll just get started on this floor then," he said, dragging the mop across the gym floor with exaggerated strokes. "Wouldn't want to interrupt your... important work."

Beside me, Mel stifled a laugh, and I gave her a look that was equal parts mortified and amused.

"We'll just get out of your way then," I said, desperately trying to keep my voice steady as I tugged her toward the door.

As we stumbled toward the exterior doors, I shot a glance at her, my heart still racing. We both fell into an odd, stunned silence, each of us trying to regain some kind of control, like two kids caught sneaking candy before dinner.

But as soon as the warm afternoon air hit us, the absurdity of it all struck. A bark of laughter escaped my lips, and Mel joined in until we were both caught in a fit of giggles.

The tension, the awkwardness, all of it melted away as the ridiculousness of the moment took over. The fits of laughter went on and on, echoing through the empty parking lot and filling the air around us.

Finally, chuckles faded, and I was struck by Mel's beauty. Her face flushed from laughter, and her eyes sparkling with love.

We stood there for a moment, both of us still grinning even as the tension thickened between us with every passing second, the laughter replaced by a soft hum of electricity.

The air around us grew charged. It wasn't just the kiss or the near-miss with Mr. Holman; it was something deeper, something that had been building in me for a while now.

Mel's expression softening, but there was something unreadable in her eyes. She was close, but I wanted more. I wanted to step into that last inch between us.

"I guess we should really get going," I said, my voice rougher than I expected. I wasn't sure if it was the adrenaline, or the way my body still hummed from the kiss, but it felt like I was holding myself together by a thread.

Mel didn't answer right away. Instead, she took a small step forward, her fingers brushing against mine, tentative but warm. The simple touch sent a wave of heat through me.

"Yeah," she said, her voice low and teasing, "I guess we'll have to continue this experiment somewhere a little more... controlled."

I laughed, shaking my head. "Absolutely. I'm not giving up on the data."

A woman who could drop a perfect science pun after getting caught by the custodian during a make-out session? Yeah. She was definitely for me.

Mel was gravity—pulling me in, anchoring me. She was home.

I grabbed her hand and tugged her through the parking lot, our steps quickening, laughter chasing after us. By the time we reached her car, we were breathless, grinning like teenagers caught in the middle of something too good to stop.

We paused, chest to chest, breathing the same air.

"Let's go home," I whispered, the words rough with everything I meant but hadn't yet said.

Her smile was slow, sure, eyes burning with the same fire I felt in my chest. "You read my mind."

About the Author

M. Jayne LaDow combines her love of storytelling with her background as a longtime educator. When she's not creating fictional worlds where coffee is plentiful, snowstorms are romantic, and teachers always have a happy ending, you can find her at the beach, spending time with her family, or being distracted by her cats. She lives in Virginia Beach with her husband, kids, and a bunch of furry and reptilian friends.

Acknowledgements

Books by M. Jayne LaDow One Night Stands and Lesson Plans Learning Goals and Dancing Poles Pop Quizzes and Stolen Kisses Tardy Pass, No Questions Asked Coming in November 2025: A Pilgrimage of Whispered Truthsjourney. Your enthusiasm, messages, and love for Marchfield keep me going, and I'm endlessly grateful to be on this ride with you.

To Jim—thank you for your steady support and for never questioning why I'm muttering out loud or writing all day. I love it, and I love you.

To Miles and Megan—thank you for your endless patience and for answering all of my questions. Your openness has taught me more than I could ever put into words.

To Liz—thank you for being my late-night reader, loyal hype squad, and lifelong best friend. You always show up, and I never stop being grateful for it.

To Lauren—you are my sounding board, my research department, and chief brainstormer extraordinaire. These books wouldn't exist without you, bestie.

To Suzanne—thank you for keeping me focused when I'm spiraling and cheering me on when I find my flow. Your texts, check-ins, and camaraderie remind me I'm not doing this alone.

To Nancy—thank you for being an accountability partner. You always ask, you always listen, and your encouragement lands exactly when I need it.

To Erin—thank you for wrangling my chaos with grace. Your thoughtful edits and insight have made this story sharper, stronger, and more *me*. I couldn't ask for a better editor.

And to all the educators and student—thank you for the inspiration. Your courage, compassion, and ridiculous sense of humor are at the core of every character I write. You are the real heroes of Marchfield.

Stay Tuned for Something
New and Different

By M. Jayne LaDow

A Pilgrimage of Whispered Truths:

She set out to solve a mystery,

not to fall in love. In 1997 Virginia Beach, some truths refuse to stay buried...

Danica Jones is used to lesson plans and late-night grading—not murder. But everything changes when a student's angry uncle confronts her after class, only to disappear days later. On an Earth Day cleanup, Dani makes a chilling discovery: the man's body, hidden in the marsh.

Suddenly thrust into the heart of a mystery that has shaken her coastal town, Dani can't walk away—not when she was the last to see him alive.

Enter Chris Larkhurst, a smooth-talking radio newsman with his own secrets. What starts as curiosity between them soon becomes a dangerous investigation, revealing a web of greed, church arson, and buried lies.

As Dani and Chris follow the clues from boardwalk diners to forgotten chapels, their connection deepens—but trust is hard to come by when danger lurks just around the corner.

Mystery, romance, and a city full of secrets—*A Pilgrimage of Secrets* is a spicy romantic whodunit about uncovering the truth, finding love, and the unexpected lessons that change everything.

Books by M. Jayne LaDow

One Night Stands and Lesson Plans
Learning Goals and Dancing Poles
Pop Quizzes and Stolen Kisses
Tardy Pass, No Questions Asked
Coming in November 2025: *A Pilgrimage of Whispered Truths*